T0266721

"This is what small-town Ontario looks like when ~~~~~~ Attenborough is a distant memory, when social structures are as polluted as the water, when myth has returned—big time—in mounting waves, sweeping our smaller stories out to sea. I don't what is more terrifying: that The Pump exists, or that here, in this wretched, sinking place, you can find something that you desperately love, something that you want to survive. *The Pump* is an astonishing debut collection from a writer who is just warming up."

— Tom Cull, author of *Bad Animals*

"*The Pump* is populated with the kind of tough, awkward, dark, and tender characters you often find trapped in small town, no-place Canada. You'll also find beavers, salt domes, a lighthouse, marshes, more beavers, a Mercury Villager, mosquitoes, and the rest of the beavers. Hegele has woven an inescapable, ferocious dream of a book. Good luck getting out."

— John Elizabeth Stintzi, author of *My Volcano* and *Vanishing Monuments*

"Bristling with magic, horror, and romance, *The Pump* transforms small-town Southern Ontario into a place of violence and sacrifice—or maybe presents it as it truly is. Like nothing I've ever read before, these killer beavers, strange diseases, and infectious waters wouldn't leave my head and drew me back to their world again and again. If only I blurbed delightfully weird books like this for the rest of my life, I'd be happy."

— Jess Taylor, author of *Pauls* and *Just Pervs*

"This is the Southern Ontario that we don't openly acknowledge but that scrapes at the back of our memories. *The Pump* shows us the surreal violence of living in the 401's sprawl and the staggering beauty of the nature that surrounds it. Don't be fooled by the nightmarish quality of these stories: they are as real as the Mercury Villager that Sydney Hegele drives us in on. This is horror in broad daylight. These are the living ghosts that haunt so many of us who grew up here."

— Jia Qing Wilson-Yang, Lambda Award-winning author of *Small Beauty*

THE PUMP

Sydney Hegele

Invisible Publishing
Halifax & Toronto

Library and Archives Canada Cataloguing in Publication

Title: The pump / Sydney Warner Brooman.
Names: Brooman, Sydney Warner, author.
Description: Short stories.
Identifiers: Canadiana (print) 20210246391 | Canadiana
(ebook) 20210246421 | ISBN 9781988784793 (softcover) |
ISBN 9781988784823 (HTML)
Classification: LCC PS8603.R662 P86 2021 | DDC C813/.6—dc23

Edited by Annick MacAskill
Cover and portrait artwork by Jeremy Bruneel
Interior design by Megan Fildes | Typeset in Laurentian
With thanks to type designer Rod McDonald

Invisible Publishing is committed to protecting our natural envi-
ronment. As part of our efforts, both the cover and interior of this
book are printed on acid-free 100% post-consumer recycled fibres.

Printed and bound in Canada.

Invisible Publishing | Halifax & Toronto
www.invisiblepublishing.com

Published with the generous assistance of the Canada Council for
the Arts, the Ontario Arts Council, and the Government of Canada.

 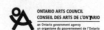

"Something happened here. In your life there are a few places, or maybe only the one place, where something happened, and then there are all the other places."

Alice Munro, "Face"
from *Too Much Happiness*

For Jakob in London.
For Olga in Heaven.
For Margaret in "Vellum."
For the ones who left The Pump.
For the ones still there.

Your mother does not want to move to The Pump. Her father's shoe store chain is based in the city, but when he knocks up his college sophomore cashier, the two of them sell the stores and take all the money with them to the States, to picnic with their kid and let him climb up the back of Confederate statues and ride them like ponies. Your grandfather leaves your mother and uncle nothing but two thousand dollars and an old fur hat.

Your mother and her brother play house in their apartment downtown. Thick walls muffle his screaming at her that she's not the Queen of Sheba and that she can reorder his *National Geographic* hardcover books *correctly* or they're gonna get shoved up her ass. She says she doesn't know the order because she can't fucking read minds, and she rips the books apart, sheet by sheet, crimson-faced and frothing at the mouth, until a pile of hardback shells covers the mouldy carpet like a deck of playing cards.

Your uncle gets tired of playing house. He plays doctor with your mother while she sleeps. Her nails dig deep into the bed frame. She prays to a God that she does not know while the doctor cures her.

In the freezing rain of a March night, your pregnant mother packs her brother's Mercury Villager and drives south. The car reeks of stale apple juice. She leaves the fur hat.

She enters the Greenbelt. The words JENNY IS A HOTTIE DANNY IS GAY are spray-painted in bright blue on the rock walls that sandwich the highway.

The first thing she notices about The Pump is the water. It gushes thick out of bathroom taps darker than dirt. It fills lemonade glasses and kiddie pools and toilet bowls and rec centre fountains. It sits full and dirty in the stomachs and lungs of stillborn bodies buried beneath the ground. The town's water filtration system is in a perpetual state of disrepair. There is an empty pumphouse at the edge of an old soccer field, used for summer camps and Scouts.

Sewage seeps through the mud up into the grass. Moon-crater sores run up your mother's arms and legs until she turns off the plumbing altogether.

Three months later, you are born in The Pump. Your first breath drips with the scent of the lake. The nurse washes you with bottled water. Your mother takes a drag from a hand-rolled cigarette and blows the smoke out like a geyser.

To the nurse's surprise, you are born alive. The other babies are born blue, mouths open in shock.

Condensation streaks the windows of the hospital room. You are named after your late grandmother Joanne. Your mother does not give you a middle name. She thinks that middle names are for princes and pedophiles.

Outside, the beavers cry like wolves.

THE BOTTOM

Ellie got given a job for once thank God [finally] she could help with the help for the first time she was so goddamn *helpful*. Daddy pricked her finger with the tip of his hunting knife and spat out li'l crunchy mosquito corpses and held the blade between his cracking teeth while he filled her palm with raisins. Her big brown eyes sucked up the sight so good. She was so damn good at looking dammit she was *so good* she could even be a looker for the mayor. Hardened marsh mud stuck between the mesh in her pink stockings and she didn't even care 'cause they were all dried-up li'l bits now. Daddy pointed to the pines on the ground behind them.

Smear the snacks good and scatter 'em into the cracks of the stumps.

Ellie ran her finger over the raisins that were bathwater fingers without the finger part. Daddy was probably hoping she would trip and drop 'em all in the water so he could run his mouth over dinner about how he *knew* she'd find a way to fuck up [the hunt].

Pussy can't follow orders for *shit*. Bodhi's only seven and he can throw a fucking raisin. I bring him out with swarms of bugs snackin' on his baby curls and he scoops up shit with his butterfly net and shoves it into his mouth like a dying hog *and he can still throw a fucking raisin*.

At least they were in the marshes and not at the green Ikea table with the plastic chairs where they were all together all alone sitting in the loud quiet. Before Mama left, she made the loud quiet like she made rosemary bread and they had to eat it up [all gone] unless they wanted to drip skin till they were gangly skeletons.

Ellie waded through the muck and put the pile of blood-covered raisins near the trees and Daddy watched her with his arms crossed all focused-like and everything. Now was the part with the waiting now was the part where you waited now was the waiting [that part]. Daddy waited for the water to boil and Daddy waited for spring for the hunt and Daddy waited for the cops to find the cabin but pigs don't have good eyesight so you just hide right in the middle right in the open air. Ellie couldn't wait one second one sentence one nothing. Bodhi would plug his ears with moss when he was small when Ellie was just a tiny little rat of a human and would cryandcryandcryandcryandcryand-cryandcryandcryandcryandcryandcryandcry and they'd leave her in a li'l basin in the mud so she really did look like a hog and the beavers would hear her wailing and they'd swim up from their li'l treasure holes like furry mermaid pirates and they'd be sniffing around [twitchin' and such in the breeze] and even lick Ellie's li'l baby face but they wouldn't eat her up like a chicken thigh 'cause Daddy would wrap 'em from behind with the fishing net and [PLOP] cut them in the head like a jack-o'-lantern.

They used the raisins now that Ellie and Bodhi were too big to be bait.

Daddy crossed an arm in front of Ellie's chest. Keep still I hear the flappin' keep *still*. We all need the hats this winter even Pussy needs a hat to keep warm. We get 'em before they get us that's what I said we get 'em before they get us.

One beaver waddled up to the stump from the darkness of the trees. Daddy clamped a hand over Ellie's mouth and Ellie looked out over the water [she was a good Looker].

She got that heavy feeling [almost like rocks but not really] that made her not want to be there anymore. She wanted home. With Mama braiding her hair and slicking it back with hard hands and cooing into her left ear do you see 'em do you see 'em? Ellie do you see the beavers? Once, her and Mama went outside in their ripped bathrobes and walked barefoot under the big big moon and into the water and called out to the beavers come on out it's okay we're all from the same place we're the same I can't skin you we're the same.

Mama looked at the baby beaver like she was looking at a dirty mirror like she was moving back and forth and waiting for it to do the same. Then she put Ellie down in the mud and walked up to it and the algae squished through the gaps between her toes and she grabbed the sides of the beaver's face and the whiskers twitched and she told it a secret. Ellie couldn't hear.

Now in the marsh the beavers didn't see them. The beavers waddled over and sniffed the raisins. They ate the little fingers up—really sucked on them like baby Ellie and her thumb.

Daddy got the net ready. The mosquitoes swerved through the holes like dumb guppies. Ellie was looking and trying to eat up the loud quiet. She wished Mama was there to coo at the beaver and to tell it the secret so it could leave [so so so fast].

Should she say that she didn't need a hat anymore? That it was too warm and she just wanted to go home and sit at the Ikea table and have Mama braid her hair and look at Bodhi eat mud and holy holy [holy] hell she wanted to step out into the marsh water and stop in the middle of the pond and stand between Daddy and the beaver.

She didn't. Time moved a little slow and a little fast and a little the same like she was dizzy but she'd felt that way before like everything was everywhere. Ellie trailed behind while Daddy hurried real slow around the pond. The beaver got up on its hind legs and gripped a raisin in its tiny claws. It nibbled the skin of the raisin so good.

Daddy was quick. One second the beaver was there on its legs eatin' the raisin all up so good and another second Daddy raised the knife and the beaver's head was split open. Like a sliced watermelon like an old paint tin with dried skin over the top [like you just wanna put your hand in]. The beaver screamed and Ellie felt it at the tops of her teeth. Daddy swished the knife back and forth in the marsh water to wash it off.

Ellie knew that now she was Ellie but with parts that were different parts that were not the same. Those parts looked at the bits of beaver and felt at ease. They felt like something had come into the world that was supposed to leave and now it left and the ground was wet and everything was balanced. The old parts of her [the parts she got from Mama] were sick and grieving and the new parts had pricks of cold down their arms—a hum of light at the top of their heads. The old parts were the parts that were the same as the beavers and the new parts knew they weren't the same. They could never be the same.

And it felt good. Not good like a fire and a slow warm dream but good enough to know it was good. Daddy skinned the beaver and Ellie watched and her mouth smiled before she could tell it to. Nothing was the matter and everything mattered [so much].

Daddy sliced an ear off the beaver and let Ellie hold it on the way home. He carried the folded pelt himself 'cause Pussy'll drop it in the water that's for damn sure. Thick air sweated out into fog as they trudged back through the mud and the pines.

Ellie sniffed the fur of the ear as she walked—felt each dark hair prickle the tip of her nose. She put her own ear up against it and she swore she could hear waves. She listened for the coos and clicks of the beavers sliding slick against the mossy rocks and gliding through the water of the deepest lake. She waited for the sound of their bodies hitting the bottom.

FOUND

In all her seventy-seven years, Beverley Bone had never seen a cat in The Pump.

It sat erect on the green splintered wood of her front porch steps and fixed her with a gaze that made her feel guilty for something she hadn't done. Its white fur was matted with dirt and Beverley had the urge to tell it to get the fuck back home and take a bath.

Beverley squinted. She wouldn't trust a cat without kittens. Even shitty Pump people pumped out shitty Pump children.

The cat coughed. Violently. A small, saliva-sheened plastic bag fell out of its mouth and onto the steps. Beverley didn't want to touch it, but she wanted to see what was inside before her wife, Camilla, did.

Camilla couldn't leave one single thing for Beverley to do first. She cut their wedding cake first; walked into their shitty Pump townhouse first; cheated first; miscarried first; lost feeling in her knees first. Beverley never got to be first. Beverley yanked the sleeve of her thick wool sweater over her wrinkled palm and picked up the bag.

There were baby teeth inside, clean and bright and newly ripped from their roots. Beverley hid the plastic bag in her bookcase, behind her collection of blank journals. She liked that the teeth were like tiny secrets all her own.

Beverley was there to greet the cat the next morning. It had a rusted wedding band between its pointed teeth.

She decided she wouldn't sell it for the rent money that her retirement cheques didn't even cover. She would keep it on the bookshelf with the baby teeth—just for her. Camilla's fingers had swelled and bulged with age to the point where she couldn't wear her own wedding band. She'd insisted that Beverley take hers off as well. They had to match.

Beverley got up at five o'clock the next morning to wait for the cat. She wrapped her legs in an old sweater while she sat on the porch. She didn't want to use any of the blankets that Camilla had knitted, scratchy and heavy and salmon pink. She would've rather been cold than use a hideous blanket like that.

The cat arrived halfway through sunrise, just as the edges of the orange clouds began to turn pink. The corners of its eyes were flecked with yellow crust. Beverley sat up against the chair and put her hand out as if she were a king receiving a kiss. What have you brought me today, cat? What secrets do you want me to know?

The cat spat out three metal bullets.

They went to the back of the bookshelf with the baby teeth and the wedding band. Beverley expected the bullets to feel heavy, but they rolled around in her hand like Monopoly pieces.

She began to stay up all night to wait for the cat. She went two entire days without sleep and ate nothing but grape-flavoured cough drops. Camilla did not notice her absence in bed.

At noon on the third day, the cat arrived walking backwards—it used its hind legs to get itself up the porch stairs. It presented a large lump of orange fur at Beverley's feet.

It took her a moment to realize that the lump was the body of another cat.

Beverley did not move. Vomit gurgled at the base of her throat. The cat purred, rubbed the side of its face against the porch railing, then sauntered back down the sidewalk.

She spent the rest of the day pounding on her neighbours' doors to ask them if they'd seen a white cat. She stopped the mail carrier in front of her house and questioned him until he dropped his bag of letters in the snow and sprinted away. She jumped in front of cars on the road and slapped hand-drawn pictures of a cat with a question mark beside it onto their windshields.

She even asked Camilla if she'd heard any meowing. Camilla just sighed a long sigh in response. I can wiggle my toes to the tune of "Birdland." I know the beat so well. Beverley? Don't you like "Birdland"? Our song?

Beverley hated jazz.

She set up an open can of tuna in a damp cardboard box on the porch to try to trap the cat. A day later, the front yard smelled of old hard fish, but the box sat untouched.

Beverley waited. She picked up the dead cat with Camilla's oven mitts and put it in the compost bin out back. She waited every morning, and the white cat never came.

A week passed. She tried to make sense of the order of the gifts and couldn't.

Beverley soaked her feet in Epsom salts while Camilla rewound the tape deck. Sarah Vaughan's voice filled the air. Beverley groaned.

Turn that shit off, Cami.

I thought you liked jazz. My favourite song is coming up—I haven't heard it in forever.

You just played it. And I've told you over and over that I hate jazz, Jesus *Christ*.

You love jazz. My favourite song is coming up—I haven't heard it in forever.

Beverley awoke one night to a high-pitched screeching and the sound of nails dragging against wood, so loud that she couldn't stop Camilla from following her outside to investigate. The two of them shuffled down their dark hallway and out the front door.

Moonlight lit the porch steps. In front of them, a beaver stood on its hind legs—the white cat dead in its mouth.

BARGES

Before the trip to the marshes, each Boy Scout leader is assigned a younger Scout to watch over. You get Maxi Mommy-Socks Miller.

The two of you get ready in the pumphouse's community room with the others. Bobby Joiner gets assigned eight-year-old Taylor Levesque. Bobby dumps Taylor's bag out on the ground in front of him and tells him to repack it. Cry about it and I'll knock your teeth out, he says. Taylor wipes his eyes and nods and cleans the saltine cracker dust off his plastic water bottle.

Bodhi Sampson doesn't show, so there aren't enough leaders for the kids. Case Jameson is assigned little Danny Kilber and Milo Riccio. You guys are gonna protect me if we run into trouble, right? Case asks. Danny and Milo giggle. Case ruffles their hair.

Maxi almost strangles himself trying to put on his bright orange sash. He weeps and makes you promise there won't be storks on the hike. You rip toilet paper sheets off a roll to wipe the snot off his face. You smile:

No storks. Promise.

Maxi says he had a dream once that he had to sacrifice his mother to a stork while he watched from a closing elevator. He starts to cry again. You cover his little head in bug spray and ask him if he knows the camp song "Barges."

No, he whispers.

You find it weird that he's never heard the song. Everyone who has ever grown up in The Pump knows "Barges." Your mom taught it to you around the same time she told you the story of the storks.

She gave you a carton of strawberry milk and took your blue-and-red Spiderman comforter out of the dryer and tucked you in and sat on the edge of your twin-sized bed—the one with the white hard plastic frame—and told you about the wicked old man who lived in the lighthouse on the beach. She told you about how he used the beacon to lure ships to the rocky cliffs so that they'd crash because the storks told him to. The storks wanted him to have a new wife and new babies. The new babies would keep him safe.

You know it's just a story but you avoid the abandoned lighthouse at the edge of the marshes just in case.

Maxi had obviously heard the same folk tale. You wonder why his mom only taught him the bad parts and not the good.

You slather his face in sunscreen, being careful not to touch the scabs near his mouth.

You roll up the giant sleeves of his Scout shirt. Yours is crisp and ironed—badges sewn in a perfect row. Your mother also ironed your socks. She gave you a backup pair in case you got your feet wet. Maxi's mom never gave him socks that fit him properly. She'd send him to Scouts on Wednesday nights in little black heel liners that didn't even reach his ankles, thin as stockings. That's why Bobby gave Maxi his nickname.

Maxi's only two badges are stuck onto his sash with duct tape. He says his mom can't sew. You tie the bottom of his Tilly hat up to his chin and sing quietly, so softly that the other Scouts don't hear you:

> *Barges, I would like to go with you, I would like to sail the ocean blue. Barges, have you treasures in your hold? Do you fight with pirates brave and bold?*

Maxi asks you who the barges are and why a family is trying to fight pirates all by themselves. You explain that barges are giant boats that ship things to different countries. You tell him to picture a blue, blue ocean every time he is scared during the hike. You tell him that storks don't like singing.

Bobby Joiner blows a plastic whistle. He pushes Taylor forward and tells the group to follow him. Taylor pulls down the brim of his hat. He looks unsure.

Danny and Milo sprint ahead of Taylor, and Case runs to keep up with them.

You line up at the back of the group so that no one will make fun of you for holding Maxi's hand.

Your hiking boots squish through dark water in the grass outside the pumphouse. Your mother even ironed your shoelaces—they sit in perfect bows atop your feet. Maxi's shoes are ripped at the soles. You gave him your extra pair of socks before the hike began.

You enter the marshes and the frogs sing. You don't swat the mosquitoes away—there's no point. The air is thick and hot and heavy.

The group stops near a pond to take a drink break. Maxi's gaze moves back and forth across the sky, searching for storks.

Bobby Joiner takes his shirt off and wraps it around his neck. He flexes in the hot sun—says something about being a *man scout*.

Taylor collects small stones and washes the dirt off them in a puddle. He separates them into groups and pretends each group is a family. Each rock family has a pebble named "the baby." The baby rocks are Taylor's favourite.

Danny Kilber trips on a root and scrapes his knee. Case breaks off from the group and brings Danny and Milo back to the pumphouse to wash the cut.

Maxi sits cross-legged in the dirt. You get down to your knees and sing as quiet as you can.

Barges, I would like to go with you...

You pause. Maxi looks up with large brown eyes. He whispers:

...I would like to sail the ocean blue.

You retie Maxi's hat and hand him your water bottle.

After another kilometre through the woods, Bobby blows his whistle. Taylor jumps at the sound and spins around. His hat falls over his eyes.

Bobby turns back to the other Scouts.

Who's ready to earn their beaver badge?

No one moves. A few boys turn their heads to one another. Bobby clears his throat. What, no brave Boy Scout volunteers? Are we a band of pussies?

He smiles at Taylor and Taylor furiously shakes his head.

Maxi turns to you.

I want a badge. I want another badge.

Don't talk.

But Bobby said we can get a—

Shut up.

You place your hand over his. You're brave without a badge, Maxi.

Bobby walks through the group. Your gaze goes to your shoes. He smiles. What about Mommy-Socks? Doesn't he want his beaver badge?

He doesn't, you interrupt.

Bobby laughs.

Oh, come on. I think the kid can speak for himself.

You lock eyes with Bobby. Maxi looks between the two of you. He stands.

I do. I do want a beaver badge.

Bobby turns to face you. He throws his arms up. Well, whattaya know. He wants the badge.

Everything speeds up. Maxi is shoved to the front of the group. His sash droops down to his knees.

You strain to see above the other boys' heads.

Bobby steps into the water and motions for Maxi to follow. He grabs hold of Maxi's shoulders. You can't hear what he's saying. He whispers to Maxi and points to the other side of the pond.

Suddenly you're pushing your way to the pond's edge. You say that you want your beaver badge instead. You want to go first.

Maxi scowls at you.

I thought you wanted me to be brave.

You know you should tell him, but he is standing tall in the blazing sun, amidst the swarms of bugs, looking as if he could confront a thousand storks and come out victorious. He's got a look in his eye like he's ready to sail the ocean blue. Maybe he'll be fine.

You step back into the group and watch.

Bobby backs up out of the water and grabs hold of Taylor's shoulders. He points to Maxi.

Watch, he says. Pay attention.

Taylor nods.

Maxi wades through dark green. Water striders dance figure eights around his little body. He stops to look back once. Twice. Bobby shouts at him to hurry up.

It happens too quickly for you to fully comprehend. You hear a flurry of movement, a high-pitched whine, and a growl. Wailing turns to choking—gurgling. A splash.

And your name. Maxi is shouting your name.

You stumble forward into the open air. You push past the other boys—shove Bobby aside—and you half-run half-fall into the water as you try to reach Maxi. You don't see him. You don't see him, but you hear the ripping.

You duck under the water. Mud clouds your vision. Your shirt is soaked. Your mom will have to iron it again.

You see the orange sash. It's floating in a cluster of reeds at the other end of the pond. The duct tape is unstuck; the badges are gone. There is no body—nothing for you to revive. Nothing for his mother to bury.

You hold the sopping sash in your arms and turn to look at the rest of the boys back across the water. Taylor is screaming. It hurts to hear him. He's dropped to his hands and knees in the mud.

Bobby's mouth is fixed into a hard line. His face is pale. For the first time, he looks back at you with fear. He looks at you like he doesn't quite understand. Neither of you really do. You are both afraid. You do not sing, instead mouth the words:

> *Taking their cargo out into the sea. How I wish someday they'd take me.*

PELARGONIA
FROM GREEK PELARGÓS (STORK)

Caroline could not get her husband hard.

A haze spread across the dark lake water in cloudy tufts and seeped through the broken bay window, thicker than the fog they normally got in the cove. She couldn't quite see him, nor he her, which made the whole ordeal that much more difficult. Wind swept chipped paint off the stone walls and into the rafters, and the bits of indigo swirled up into the lighthouse spire like snowflakes. Thirty-eight days in the sickly dark. Abe refused to turn on the beacon because the dark was the only way to get the girls—out touring the lake in their cabin-cruiser boats—to the lighthouse. He said he could practically smell the algae in the next one's hair. I'll bet she'll be smaller than the last one, he said. I'll bet her skin will be smooth like beach glass.

Caroline forced a moan from the back of her throat. Tell me more about her, she said to Abe. What songs does she sing while your baby drifts off to sleep? How damp are your palms clamped against her lips as you fuck her?

She smiled and stretched her arms upward in a way she thought he would find alluring.

Nothing. Abe sighed and rolled off the bed. As he walked to the window, he bumped into the bassinet. The damp plush pad reeked of mildew and aged urine.

We can try again. Abe. We can try ag—

She'll be here soon.

The storks told Abe that the woman would come within the week—and so she did.

Her arrival was a birth: loud and righteous, bloody and hopeful. Caroline heard the screech of metal against the rocks of the cove and saw dark smoke pluming up through the haze.

She could not see Abe below but knew that he was pulling the girl out of the ship wreckage and onto the slime of a large rock; taking his bright yellow rain jacket off and draping it over her shoulders as she coughed up half the lake—carefully leading her up the wooden spiral staircase. Let's get you something warm. All that hair—you could be a mermaid. Our very own mermaid.

Caroline boiled raspberry leaves and bottled water, set out three chipped mugs with hand-painted anchors on the sides. The woman came into the loft wearing Abe's slickers. She was smaller than the last one—drowning in the dripping jacket. Stringy blond hair clung to her neck in matted knots. Caroline had hoped that she would be blond. The blond ones gave them more time.

The girl said her name was Lyssa. Caroline opened a can of sardines for her and she slurped each fish up like soup—scraped the sauce out of her fingernails with her teeth. She asked why they didn't just eat fish from off the cove. Abe laughed too loudly for too long. I wouldn't even stand in the rain in that liquid shit. Let those cyclops salmon fuck each other. Fuck 'em.

She thanked them for the food. Folks just don't care anymore, you know? Bringing me into your own place like that, just having it here, it's a miracle really.

Abe said that the only reason they even had a home was because of hospitality, so he felt the need to pay it forward. The storks keep us safe from the water—we keep them fed, and they keep us safe.

She nodded as if she understood.

Abe gave Lyssa drinks in dusty green bottles. He told her about the time the crabs showed up dead on the shore, but then a stork arrived the next morning at daybreak with a basket of fresh ones and Caroline spilled them out onto the wooden loft floor and watched them fumble around in confusion as if they didn't understand that they were crabs. After they'd eaten their fill, they speared the extra ones with the sharpened end of a broomstick just for the fun of it. Lyssa howled with laughter.

Caroline sat Lyssa down on her bed in a dry nightgown and explained the conditions of the arrangement. Abe paced outside the door. Some of the girls hadn't agreed, which made things that much more difficult, but Lyssa did not want to be difficult. Caroline smiled and ran a hand through Lyssa's drying hair. Even as the sky outside blackened, the haze only seemed to spread further, sticking to the bay window like a captured cloud.

Caroline went back to the kitchen while Abe and Lyssa fucked in the bedroom.

Lyssa started puking up bile every sunrise and suddenly couldn't bear the smell of cooked fish. She scrubbed shells under boiled bottled water and caressed her stomach, barely budging yet. I feel like he's going to be big, she'd say. Huge, like he's already six years old and is just crouching in there for warmth. Bigger than your last one maybe.

Abe shot her a glare over his cup of coffee.

You'd better hope so.

Months passed and the haze continued to thicken. Caroline and Lyssa lay out like rotting fish on the largest cliffside rock and baked themselves in the sun. Caroline propped her elbows up onto Lyssa's growing belly and read aloud from an old book of fairy tales she thought that the baby would like:

> *But the naughty boy, who began the song first, what shall we do to him? cried the young storks.*
>
> *There lies in the pond a little dead baby who has dreamed itself to death, said the mother.*
>
> *We will take it to the naughty boy, and he will cry because we have brought him a little dead brother. And the boy who said it was a shame to laugh at animals, we will give him a little brother and sister, too, because he was good.*

Lyssa swelled faster than the last girl—larger—her belly button peeking out of one of Abe's flannel shirts. Her walk became a waddle.

The ninth month came to an end and Abe began to grind his teeth together till they chipped. Caroline drank the water straight from the kettle and let out a sigh as it scorched her tongue.

Sometimes Caroline thought about keeping it—just in the quiet moments. She thought about running away with Lyssa, somewhere, to the marshes, maybe. She could brush Lyssa's pretty blond hair and braid it down her back before they took the baby to see the beavers.

One morning, a heavy rain swept through the cove and Caroline left the kettle screaming until the metal softened. Abe shoved his empty mug forward, but she just stared back at him. Do you like it here, Abe? I mean, how much do you really like it? The lighthouse?

He pushed his chair aside and gripped her jaw tightly—pulled her face right up against his so that Lyssa wouldn't hear them speak.

You wanna go back out? Out there?

No...no, I just meant—

Go the fuck ahead. Go make love to the mermaids, Care—cuddle all your fucking babies right into the lake and use them as a raft for the rest of your short, miserable life.

He stormed off, back up into the spire. Caroline could still feel the heat of his fingers on her chin.

The baby came at night. A starless black sky swaddled her quiet entrance into the world.

Caroline cut the cord with a paring knife and clutched the baby's tiny body—wiped blood off her forehead with an old towel and held her ear against the baby's chest, just to hear the thump of her little heartbeat—like listening for the life of the ocean inside a shell. One of the girls from two years earlier had told her that the sounds in shells were only the echo of your eardrum—just your own life reflected back to you.

Lyssa lay sprawled out on the wicker couch with a cold cloth around her neck. Pupils swallowed her eyes. Is it time yet, Abe? Is it here? Is it time?

Abe glanced at Caroline and made a forward motion with his hand.

Give it to me. You go turn on the beacon.

Caroline froze. She clutched the baby hard enough to leave fingernail marks in her soft skin. Abe's gaze shifted to a glare.

Caroline. The beacon.

Lyssa kept her glazed eyes up on the spire above them. Is it time? Is it time yet, Abe? Is it time?

Caroline backed up toward the bay window—shifted the baby to her left arm.

Is it time yet, Abe? Is it time yet?

And suddenly she was running, faster than she knew her feet could carry her, pushing through the wooden door and stumbling down the spiral staircase four steps at a time. She could hear Abe's panicked steps and Lyssa's screams reverberating off the stone. The baby began to shriek and Caroline clutched her tighter—sprinted desperately until the night air hit her face and the bottoms of her bare feet felt the slick wet of cliffside stone.

She could barely see the difference between rock and water. Everything melted together. The rain blurred her vision. A funnel of light from the beacon tore through the sky.

The door knocker slammed. Abe stood a foot from her, dripping with sweat.

Caroline—

We could go to the marshes.

Give me the *fucking* baby.

She looked back at Abe with tired eyes, then looked back at the cliffside. She padded toward the water until her toes curled over the edge of the rock. The baby wailed.

Fine, then—do it. We'll make another. There'll be more. You'll be dead and there'll be more.

Dawn was breaking. She pictured her body falling. The image made her feel a blissful calm.

Wind pushed Caroline back from the cliffside. A flash of white—the flurry of feathers—the crunch of bone—and Caroline's arms were suddenly empty.

She did not drop her arms until the stork was gliding high above her. Angelic white wings spanned metres. Abe smiled as he walked over the rocks to Caroline and pulled her tightly against his chest. Her neck tensed against his bearded face. His eyes closed in the embrace, but Caroline kept hers open. She watched over Abe's shoulder as the stork passed over the top of the lighthouse and began its journey home—its long orange beak speared through the baby's broken neck. Her little limp legs dangled against the red of the rising sun.

VELLUM

Eloise caught the rash from her brother in early winter, but she didn't get the urge to write on herself until February. The small red bumps on her arms hardened, darkened, and spread. Her body moulted. Then there was an itch in her brain—an idea she couldn't ignore: *write more*.

At first Eloise only used skin that had already dried and fallen off. But as the rash progressed, she peeled it off herself in strips. Snowflakes melted into rain on the morning she decided to rip off her left thumbnail.

That morning's word was *ineffable*. Each word or phrase carried a different feeling. *Ineffable* was thick and fluttery and delicious. She needed to write it down.

She dislodged the nail and wrote the word with a thin-tipped Sharpie. After that came the shock, a pulsing pain of little heartbeats. She hid the nail on the floor behind her bookcase.

Eloise didn't even know what *ineffable* meant. Bodhi said it once when the two of them were small, back when he used their mother's old books to teach the beavers in the marshes how to read. He swore they could understand him when he spoke. He made decent progress until Ed made them keep every book in the kitchen cupboard so they could use the pages as fire starters. When money ran dry, the pages became everything from toilet paper to meat packaging. Their stepmom, Lisa, once used half a Bible and cornstarch to make a cast for Bodhi after Ed cracked his wrist in two just to prove he could.

Eloise wrapped her thumb with a dictionary page and left to meet Margaret in the parking lot of Mr. Desperate's. Falling snow sifted through grey sky and over the front yard. The clouds stretched out in thick lines. Asphalt-covered ice chunks sat squat in the dead grass that lined the driveway. Everything blistered.

Margaret was feeding Jo Lionel's scraggly white cat pieces of a fruit-and-nut chocolate bar when Eloise got there. Jo's cat was one of the only cats in The Pump.

Margaret's hair was clipped back into a red ball cap. Pine needles littered the ground and stuck to the bottom of Eloise's boots.

Margaret took something small and shiny out of her pocket and gave it to the cat. It took Eloise a moment to realize it was a ring. The cat took the ring between its teeth and ran off. Margaret always had to make her story more interesting. Eloise was used to it.

Margaret turned to Eloise. She struggled to speak over the wind.

I don't know if I can date someone who only has nine fingernails.

Are you breaking up with me?

No, she said. It's just a thought. A working-out-of-things. I'm thinking about it, is all. I want you involved in the process.

Eloise told her she'd cover her fingers. She'd buy the gloves that miners wear—thick like rocks. She'd paint her other nine nails with Lisa's bright blue nail polish.

It's your *thumb*nail. It's a big deal.

Eloise felt pain ripple through her tongue. She clenched her jaw.

Margaret walked away and the cat followed.

Later, Eloise peeled a strip of skin off her left calf. When it dried, she wrote on it with her black marker:

> *Pine needles. Margaret was angry today. It hurt and I loved it.*

She blew softly on the sentence to keep the marker from smudging. She put the strip behind the bookshelf with the others.

Eloise chewed a plastic bottle cap while her stepmom, Lisa, left the dishes to soak and ran her mouth about the government.

Bodhi won't bother with water soon enough, Lisa said, not like water is all that special or anything. Bodhi isn't all that special either, we're all just ants here you know, and the Q101 news said last night, the one at eight with that blond slut and her geometry tattoos, they said the water down here in The Pump ends up being *toxic* for the *mind* for *people* like *them*, for Bodhi, with the rash. They can stop it any time they want to, you know, that's what Mayor Jameson says, but they think the wet is actually living, like it's microaneurysms or something, and that it's giving them false hope that they're gonna be okay, but they'll get maggots soon enough, the lot of them. I mean, they can stop it if they want to, but we shouldn't be giving them something to make them think anything's going to go away, and that Bodhi don't wanna be lied to.

I'm not lying to anyone, Eloise said.

Mayor Jameson's talk about the water always rubbed Eloise the wrong way. Jameson's wife and both of his parents had died of the rash a few years back, but even that couldn't get him to admit there was a problem.

Eloise was a freshman at Lakeside Secondary when Bohdi and Mayor Jameson's son Case were both seniors. When Case's mom died, Bodhi insisted he and Eloise go to the wake to pay their respects, even after Ed said they weren't allowed anywhere near those cunts, even in death.

Bodhi snatched a robe tie and wore it in one big knot around his neck like a scarf. Eloise put on her sluggers. She didn't think going barefoot would be appropriate.

The wake was held in the hall at St. Joseph's. Bodhi and Eloise hid at the back behind the white flower display. They ate cream-cheese pinwheels and drank Earl Grey tea until they felt like puking. Case spotted Bodhi, and the two of them ducked out through the back door and went to smoke Benson & Hedges in the cemetery. Eloise could join so long as she didn't rat them out.

The boys sat at the steps of the Miller family's crypt and argued about the ethics of killing their fathers while Eloise lay in the dead grass and made clicking noises to attract baby deer.

Fine, but like, what if your dad was a killer? Case asked. Like Bernardo? What if he kidnapped little girls and shit?

Case took a drag and coughed until his eyes watered. Bodhi lit them a new butt.

Is he *like* Bernardo or *is he* Bernardo?

Like. Still your real dad but killed a few people. Not in jail yet—still out killing.

Bodhi shrugged. Depends on who he killed.

Case tapped his foot against the ground while he considered Bodhi's point.

Your sister, Case said finally. He clasped his hands together like a gun and pointed at Eloise. He flicked his wrist. Pow.

Eloise went limp and fell backwards into the grass as dramatically as she could. I'm so dead! she screamed. The deadest! I'm the deadest one who ever lived!

Bodhi laughed and rolled his eyes. Nope. Still wouldn't kill him.

You're fucking with me, Case said. You would totally do it. You would have to.

He's my dad, Bodhi said. What, like you'd do it?

Damn right, Case said. I'd do it if he wasn't a killer. I'd do it right now.

Case held out the cigarette to Eloise.

Eloise glanced at Bodhi and waited for his nod before taking it. She sucked the filter soggy. The boys laughed.

What's stopping you then? Bodhi asked Case. Why not off him?

'Cause he'd fucking kill me, Case said.

But he'd already be dead.

And then his ghost would come back and keep me on a leash, Case said. And I'd die of fucking boredom even slower than I already am.

What's so bad about being bored? Eloise wondered.

Bodhi nodded like he understood, even though he didn't.

Eloise hadn't seen Case since—except on TV.

Lisa continued her rant out loud to no one while Eloise went out to the porch to prep flyers for her paper route. The grocery coupons and copies of the paper arrived each morning before sunrise, bundled in separate piles with twine and a single zip tie. Eloise broke the zip tie with her teeth and stuffed one flyer per paper. After a pile of ten or so, she put the stack in her green Fisher-Price wagon with the cracked plastic wheels and started again. She did this until the wagon was full.

Bodhi gave her the route after he dropped out of school and started helping Ed with the hunt full-time. She used to help him carry the papers when the snow came, before they had a wagon to put them in. Back when they trudged around in soaked sneakers and open windbreakers and no gloves. They'd waited under the stop sign at Brooker Street and Baily Avenue where they knew the older kids with wagons came on their routes. Sixteen-year-old giants against an eight-year-old Bodhi.

Bodhi would walk right up to the older boys as if he weren't two feet shorter, glaring with heat while Eloise watched from the hedges. His hands trembled.

Gimmie one of the wagons.

The boys looked at each other smugly. Bodhi's voice cracked.

Are you—are you deaf? The wagon. Gimme a wagon—a *fucking* wagon.

A pause. The boy's winter breath came out in short puffs.

Fine, kid. It's yours.

It didn't always go this well. Sometimes fists full of Bodhi's shirt, sometimes their screaming faces so close he could feel their spit hit his skin. It never deterred him. They couldn't do anything worse than Ed.

The boys left. Bodhi grabbed the wagon handle.

Ellie—get in so they don't flop all over the place. No, like this. Hold on so you don't fall out.

She figured the whole city could hear her laughter as she toppled forward into the papers with each bump in the sidewalk. The stack fell into her lap and covered her tiny body.

Bodhi walked backwards and yanked the wagon forward an inch at a time with both his hands so he could talk to her while they went the long way around the construction zone. I—I'm sorry. I'm sorry, Ellie.

She looked at Bodhi as if he were a god—glistening sweat and commanding stature and everything that would keep her safe.

Suddenly, Eloise felt like she had to check on Bodhi. She likened it to watching a sleeping cat, anxiously waiting for it to inhale to ensure it wasn't dead. She put the papers down halfway through stuffing and went inside.

She jumped down three steps at a time to his basement bedroom. The light switch at the bottom shocked her when she touched it. Mouldy comic book pages curled at her feet. She could feel him against the door like when they were younger. She hadn't seen him since his lips had peeled off a month earlier, but she remembered the way he'd puffed out his cheeks like a fish to make her laugh, even through his pain.

She knocked twice. Shuffling. A moment later, Bodhi pushed something flat and dry under the door and onto her side. Part of his palm. Two words. *Stop writing.*

After she finished stuffing the papers, she took the strip of skin up to her bedroom and read it over and over again until she fell asleep. Jo Lionel's cat scratched in desperation at her broken window screen through the night.

Hers spread faster than Bodhi's. They'd always done everything at the same pace, but the Rash treated her differently than it treated him. He liked haiku. Her words grew into paragraphs and lodged into her ears until she picked off the skin and wrote them out. The scabs began to spread and scar before new words even arrived.

One morning, after she'd clipped a square of thigh skin onto her curtain rod to dry, Margaret called and cried and said that the Tuesday sun hurt her eyes too much for her to go to work. She asked if Eloise would cover her shift at the pioneer village after school camp, and could she bring Margaret's pot-bellied pig with her. Margaret said she needed quiet time.

I love European Birch, Eloise said, pronouncing each syllable of the pig's name so that she didn't accidently call it *bitch*. She hated pigs but missed Margaret's fingers. When she lost her own, she wondered if Margaret would open things for her. Like bags of chips.

European Bitch squirmed and slathered sweat and coarse hair onto the front of Bodhi's jean jacket when Eloise picked him up. She gripped him tight for the long walk and explained how angry Margaret made her. She told him so she wouldn't have to write it down.

When she got to the Cultural Centre, she poured out the rest of her water bottle into a Tupperware container swiped from the staff room for European Bitch and locked him in the pioneer village chapel. She took a second outside the wooden door and prayed that the pig wouldn't die of heat exhaustion before she returned.

She went into the backroom of the gallery and changed into a long grey pleated skirt with burn marks—from that time that she thought she could iron—and a white button-down blouse. The words burned. Somewhere outside, a little boy screamed that he had seen a bee, and another kid accused him of lying.

Marty Miller shouted from outside the door. One of the campers' moms wants to know where her son's popsicle stick is. The one he left here three weeks ago. She's sure we didn't look properly last time. Look again, she says. She doesn't have all day, she says, they have hip-hop camp at nine forty-five. They live an hour and a half, two hours, they live three hours away, she says. Do you even know how much gas costs? Do you even know what the Liberals did to gas prices?

Eloise peeled off skin from the inside of her elbow, wrote *Gas prices—Liberals* on it, and flattened it out inside her phone case. She stuffed her sleeve with white napkins.

The kids sat in a lopsided circle on the schoolhouse floor, sucking their mittens and licking slices of store-bought cornbread before crushing them in their palms. Eloise passed around a mason jar of buttermilk and let them each shake it wildly until it became a greasy monstrosity that sort of resembled butter. Mary Shaw admitted that she was lactose intolerant and began to weep.

Eloise thought about how Bodhi used to fill dollar-store plastic bags with expensive cornflakes and coffee creamer, stolen for her in elementary school because he knew how much she wanted cereal for lunch instead of nothing at all.

The bag sat in her denim backpack all day and the warm liquid would seep into her ringed notebook pages. The book smelled faintly like sour milk every time she went to practise her daily times tables. She smirked proudly at lunch hour and gloated to Bobby Joiner and Danny Kilber that she had a brother who made her breakfast whenever she wanted—slurped it up through a bite mark in the bottom corner because only children subjected to the harsh rule of helicopter parenting were forced to wield utensils. The cereal softened and congealed into a lumpy mass and Eloise ate it all, spoiled creamer flowing down her chin.

Bodhi got caught stealing the creamer on the Eggs & Things security cam once, and the pigs brought him home even though he probably would've been safer in county jail. The cruiser was barely out of the driveway before Ed backed Bodhi up against the kitchen wall and pressed the barrel of a rimfire rifle against his forehead.

Do you love me, you little shit? Ed screamed. I'll know if you're lying. You tell me right now.

I love you, Bodhi whispered between sobs. I'm not lying. I love you. I'm sorry. I love you.

Eloise watched Ed drag Bodhi across the kitchen floor by his hair. She heard Bodhi beg not to be locked out in the dark. Blood poured from his nose onto the concrete of the front steps.

One of the kids shrieked and Eloise returned to here and now. Devin Anderson was up on the windowsill, mouth and nose pressed against the glass. Look, in the river. *Look*. It's a beaver, lookit. I saw it first—it's a *beaver*.

Chaos. Tiny bodies stumbled and sprinted outside onto the frosted grass, rushing to get a look at the beaver. Eloise could tell from the schoolhouse steps that it was dead. Necks craned in desperation to see the body on the riverbank.

Moira Wendell stroked the beaver's limp tail and screamed. A kid whose name Eloise had forgotten wouldn't stop saying *rabies*. Wind rippled through the fur like breath.

Eloise remembered zipping through the groves of dead saplings in the marshes at their old house, sharp twigs catching her cheeks and scratching the skin as she sprinted after her brother. Soaked socks and large rain boots filled with bits of acorn shells.

Bodhi. Let's be beavers and you can run the bank and I can be the beaver lady who buys sticks at the beaver store.

Can I take care of your beaver babies? Can I teach them to write French?

No. Bodhi, just no. I'm a widow who has more sticks than she knows what to do with. I exchange them at the bank so I can buy expensive bourbon for my ladies' book club. *You're* the banker.

Okay, Ellie.

Piles of birch and broken pine branches became their makeshift shop. Eloise slapped her palms on top of the pond water. She splashed through striders.

Algae caked their fingernails. They stuck bark shards down cracks in the dirt ground, baked dry by the sun. Damp shade. Birdsongs they'd try to whistle later but would never remember.

Eloise got burrs caught deep in her thick auburn hair. Bodhi sawed locks of it off with the dull Swiss Army knife he'd stolen from the church camp lost-and-found. Sorry—I gotta cut them out, Ellie, don't be a pussy. Daddy would rip 'em out. Really yank 'em. Like a chainsaw starter rope. Hold still.

She felt like Bodhi and the beavers were the same: both groups needed sticks for their houses; both did what they could to keep dry when the wind began to chill; both just wanted their own space. A safe place.

Even in winter, the body smelled. Marion Gilly took her pink toque off and placed it gently over one of the dead beaver's ears.

We should put him back in his house.

No.

But, Miss El, there's bugs.

Leave it be.

She thought that if she looked at it long enough—really carved it into the backs of her eyelids—she'd always remember the gloss in its gaze. The ripple of skin under thinning hairs. The smell. She would never forget, so she would never need to write it down. A fly walked across the beaver's wet eye. Eloise swore she saw footprints.

The scabs stopped drying. Purple soaked through every jacket sleeve. It stained socks, books, box springs, and locks of her own hair.

Eloise woke up screaming in the middle of the night, reeking like infection, sweat stinging raw patches on her neck. Lisa came in without knocking. She set a cup of chamomile on the floor beside the bed.

I was up anyway—you know how the bugs get. The damn Pump.

Eloise did know. Horseflies were avid readers.

Did I wake Ed?

No. He's out in the marshes—a beaver hunt, I guess, like those ones he used to bring you out on. It's dangerous in the dark, you know, with all those teeth, rows of 'em, not that any beaver wouldn't...well, not that they wouldn't—

Be afraid. Of Ed.

Lisa smiled as if she hadn't quite heard what Eloise had said.

I brought you water, too. Nothing fancy, just from the tap. That lady said on the TV—

I know what she said.

Lisa's eyes drained—went blank. She left without closing the door.

Margaret started calling.

At first, the messages asked for things back. Then they became warnings that she was coming by to drop off things of Eloise's, like the scrunchie Margaret had made her out of the thong she got on her sixteenth birthday, lace unwound at the sides. Sunday-morning sex echoed in her eardrums when she put it on, she claimed. I can't just wear sex in my hair if I'm trying to date again, you know. That's fucked up.

The next week, boxes of items that didn't even belong to Eloise began to show up on her front lawn. Packages of partially eaten Boston-cream-pie-flavoured chewing gum; glasses frames shaped like hearts; a large wooden placard with the price tag still attached—the words *To Thine Own Self Be True* painted across it in hot pink script.

Eloise tore skin. She wrote more. Margaret called until Eloise picked up. I don't want to interrupt your creative process. I'd just like to read some of it, is all. Your work. Not by myself, *obviously*. You'd read it to me. If you want.

Eloise ignored Margaret and everyone else. On the thirteenth, she walked all the way to the cove and back. She dragged her feet through slush and decided that all of it could hurt a little less. She would stop thinking about things that weren't herself. She would not need to write.

Eloise walked past her street. She walked all the way up Elizabeth, down Main, and past the pumphouse, to the municipal offices at the edge of town.

She had forgotten that Marty Miller's mother was Jameson's secretary. Mrs. Miller glanced at Eloise and went back to her work.

Eloise cleared her throat. Mrs. Miller did not look up.

Hi, Eloise said.

Welfare cheques don't come in till Tuesday, hun, Mrs. Miller said.

I'm here to see Case, actually.

Who?

Castor. Castor Jameson.

Valentines go in the tissue box there. Mrs. Miller pointed to her left. A reply is not guaranteed.

I need to see him, Eloise said. Like, see him see him. In real life.

Do you have a friend whose parents pay their cable bill?

I need to *talk* to him.

Don't we all, Mrs. Miller said. He's occupied.

Eloise heard a door open to her left.

Case popped his head out of the closest office. He smiled at Eloise.

Ellie, he said.

He'd grown a few inches since she'd last seen him, but he somehow looked smaller. His clothes were pressed and bright, but his dark hair looked unwashed. Purple bags puffed beneath his eyes. He looked a decade older than he was.

Eloise walked past the front desk and over to Case, who ruffled her hair. Mrs. Miller scowled.

Guilt bubbled in her stomach the moment she entered his office. Leather chairs. Old wood. A framed high school diploma. Her skin itched.

Then she noticed the glass ashtrays. Two on his desk. Three on the bookcase. One overflowing on the windowsill. One on the coffee table. One on the side table. The room coughed.

Case offered her a seat in a black leather armchair. She sat cross-legged on the ground instead.

Eloise broke the silence.

Bodhi—

I heard.

Oh, Eloise said.

You too? Case asked.

Yeah, Eloise said.

More silence. Another itch.

Did anything help? Eloise asked.

With what?

With your mom.

Case paused.

Do you mean help like, helped her while she was sick, or help like, helped me after she croaked?

Bodhi's not dead, Eloise said.

I know.

Then why the fuck did you say that?

I don't know.

Eloise stood up.

Fuck you, she said.

Case flexed his fingers. Why are you even here? he asked.

Eloise didn't answer because she didn't know.

The water, Case said finally.

What?

The water, he repeated. Don't let Bodhi drink from the tap. You shouldn't either. The water's making it worse.

You're gonna give me that bullshit? Eloise asked. You sound like my stepmom.

Fucking listen, Eloise, Case snapped. The water, got it? Stop drinking the fucking water.

Okay, Eloise said.

Repeat it back to me.

Christ, I won't touch the water. Are you done?

One more thing.

I'm all fucking ears.

Leave, Case said. Soon.

How? Eloise asked. With what money? Where the fuck would I go?

Case looked confused, and Eloise was glad. It gave her comfort knowing that he didn't understand, and probably never would.

Eloise went down to the basement when she got home. She kneeled in front of Bodhi's bedroom door and knocked once. Twice.

I saw Case today, she said, and we can't drink the tap water anymore and Margaret won't stop calling me and your jacket's all purple... your favourite one... I'm sorry.

No answer. She knocked again.

Bodhi, she said. I didn't write anything today. I think we can get better.

She kept knocking.

Bodhi.

And then she knew he was gone. The truth held her head underwater. She clawed at her throat and gasped for air. She couldn't take a full breath. She didn't know pain like that existed. She didn't know.

Eloise found Lisa smoking in the living room. She looked at Lisa and Lisa looked at her.

Where's my dad? Eloise whispered.

Out back, Lisa said. Digging.

Eloise took the rimfire rifle out of the kitchen cupboard. She loaded it slowly, just like Ed had shown her when she was little. She sat at the kitchen table and waited for him.

The wooden spindles of the armchair dug into her spine. Breathing took work. She couldn't remember the colour of Bodhi's eyes—whether they'd been Ed's or their mother's. Her body peeled while she waited. Sloughs of browned and reddened skin flaked off like leaves, wet with rot. She waited.

She waited.

The door opened. She raised the rifle.

Ed looked at Eloise and sighed. He walked to the table and sat in the chair across from her. His dirt-caked nails tapped the tabletop. She kept the gun on him.

Don't look at me like that, he said.

Eloise stretched the rifle out further. She rested the barrel against the centre of Ed's chest.

He did it himself, he said. They're saying that people can stop if they want to.

Who's saying? Eloise asked.

He coughed. Wet and full, like choking.

Everyone is.

A pause.

You doing it, too? he asked.

She nodded.

The two of them sat with the same slouch. He looked down at the pile of her skin on the ground.

The beavers'll come for that, you know, he said.

Eloise said nothing.

Ed took the barrel of the gun in his hand and held it up against his forehead.

You just gonna fuck around some more or are you gonna do it?

Eloise's hands shook.

I'm gonna leave, she stammered. I'm leaving. I'm not staying here.

Ed laughed.

Oh yeah? Where the fuck you gonna go, Ellie?

Shut it or you're dead.

Where you gonna go?

Eloise sobbed. She loosened her grip on the rifle. She let Ed yank it out of her hands and drop it onto the kitchen floor.

Ed stood up.
That's what I thought.
Then she was alone.

On Valentine's Day, Margaret called and asked if she and Eloise could break up again.

Last time wasn't very private. And I didn't say enough. We could make it more intimate. A better story.

Eloise agreed. She wrapped duct tape around her raw knuckles and left to make the trek downtown.

Margaret wanted a hot bath, so they took one, letting the water run until it reached a lighter shade of brown. Eloise and Margaret laid opposite each other in Margaret's claw-foot porcelain tub. Eloise itched her wrist over and over and Margaret pretended not to notice.

What are you thinking about?

About your brother—it's just so tragic. And how much prettier I'd be with a boy's name. Is that sexist?

Margaret's voice made the sentence sound like that part in a jazz song where the vocalist sings noises. She reached into a takeout container floating in front of her with soapy fingers and piled a handful of lo mein noodles into her mouth.

I don't know, Eloise said.

She wondered how long saliva could survive in another person's mouth. She wondered if hers was breaking down Margaret's Chinese food.

When you write about this, you'll give me a better name, right? I mean, you obviously will, right?

Her gaze settled on Eloise's scabs.

I'd like to be meaner than this. I don't have the energy right now, but you can make me meaner, right? I mean, it's sexy and all, in the bath, but it's also *so* mean to do it right here because I'm rejecting you in all your openness. You're baring it all out to me and I'm refusing you, but it's also sexy.

I guess so.

It's obviously the best thing. For your art. Heartbreak is just so much. You'll write about it for the rest of your life. Your *life*. I'll be in your biography.

It's hurting me, you know. The writing.

Wait, not just *in* your biography—the dedication. I want the dedication.

The lukewarm water wrinkled Eloise's fingertips. Dark layers of dead skin rolled up as she rubbed her arms. She imagined her brother sinking into muddy water. She read somewhere that beavers were vegetarians—but they would never be able to resist *him*. They'd be crowded around a log at the centre of their pool, fighting for a place at the table, flossing their teeth with his words.

They walked to the marshes through thick darkness. Margaret's boots shifted with her steps. She took them off and sank her feet into the damp moss. Eloise let the dirty water flood into her sneakers and soak her socks. A haze hid the moon and dulled the sheen of slick frost on the sapling branches. The beavers shrieked. Their raw throats sang for the dead.

Eloise stepped into a deep crater of ice, and green water rose to her ankles.

Margaret—let's pretend we're beavers.

Eloise scooped the mud up in her hands and let it sit in her scarred palms, heavy and cold. Her fingers didn't feel like her own—they felt as if they could fall off into the murky water one by one and she would hardly notice. She shuffled forward in the thick sludge until the mud swallowed her calves and water slopped over her knees. Margaret stood beneath an uprooted maple tree and picked at the bark. Eloise turned and shouted.

Margaret. *Margaret.*

Do you love me more than you loved your brother? Margaret asked.

Margaret's gaze narrowed through the haze. Her lips trembled. Eloise took five slow steps back toward Margaret and tripped. She gasped when the freezing water splashed against her waist.

Margaret shouted again.

Eloise. It's important.

Eloise stepped back up onto firmer ground and walked until she was an inch from Margaret's nose. Dark water dripped from her jeans.

Margaret moved to back up, but Eloise cupped her face with her dirty hands. Her fingers pressed through the mud to Margaret's cheeks.

Yes, Eloise lied, I love you more.

The mud left dark handprints. Margaret opened her mouth to speak, but Eloise had already turned around, moved back through the mud, back into the marsh. She did not feel the edges of her hair hardening into icicles as the water passed her chest. She did not feel the scrape of the logs against her ankles. She did not feel the sting of her dead skin wrinkling, wet, peeling off. She did not see it curling up and floating among the chunks of half-melted ice sheets.

Margaret craned her neck to watch.

Eloise walked. The outline of her body blurred against the dark. Bodhi was out in the water somewhere. The breath spooling out the top of the beaver dam was his.

It started snowing. Flakes caught in Margaret's thick blond curls and she did not wipe them away. She let them halo her head in white light while the beavers screamed and tears spilled down her muddy cheeks and the marshes became nothing but a dense black backdrop.

Margaret smiled. The Pump swallowed Eloise whole.

GROUNDERS

Mac Levesque told his wife that they were going to play grounders—so they did. She didn't want to offend Mac. Last time Annie said no to Mac, she had to clean their pet kitten Mr. Biscotti off the driveway with a J Cloth and Windex. After that, Annie cried every time she saw a stray but shut the fuck up when she was told to. After that, she never disagreed with Mac.

On the night of the game, they left Taylor with a sitter. Mac stood in front of the entryway mirror retying his tie while Annie knelt on the carpet and ran her hand along the top of Taylor's stuffed beaver. Mac snapped his fingers and pointed to the front door.

Out. We're already late.

Annie didn't move. She drew the stuffed beaver in close and took in a deep breath to see if she could smell her son. Mac scoffed.

Annie—now.

She let go of the stuffie and wiped streaked mascara from her cheek.

They drove downtown. Mac steered with one hand while the other rested in Annie's lap. She fiddled with his cufflink, fumbling to get it on his jacket sleeve.

Forget about everything, Mac said. All of it. Focus on me. Us. It's you and me. We're all that matters.

We're all that matters, Annie repeated.

Mac curled his hand down to squeeze his wife's knee. She flinched.

They arrived at the mayor's office building and joined the rest of the party on the top floor. Ashley Miller took their bags at the door.

Mayor Jameson had gutted the whole floor for this year's fundraiser. A reno team had ripped up the speckled grey carpet and installed a dark cherry hardwood floor. Two wraparound bars stocked with expensive liquor and new glassware replaced the usual accordion cubical dividers. Jameson's private office became a coat check. Money made the mundane space magical, though he wouldn't witness the finished product. Jameson put on the parties but never attended them. On party nights, he let his deputy mayor, Mac Levesque, run the show. So long as they raised money, Jameson didn't ask questions.

Mac crossed the room through the crowd to talk to the Kilbers. Annie followed.

Lionel Kilber laughed a deep belly laugh and slapped Mac on the shoulder. The audible smack echoed through the room. There he is, he said. Atta boy, he said. He reeked like stale sex sweat and Rogaine.

Eliza Kilber smoothed back a blond curl and smiled too widely at Annie, baring all her large white teeth. She took Annie's face in both hands and smooshed her cheeks together like a baby. Look at your skin, Eliza said. You're glowing. No, really, you are absolutely *glowing*. Are you expecting? You can tell me, you know—I wouldn't tell a soul. I swear on my mother-in-law's grave that it would be our little thing—no one else. You can tell me.

Mac kept a tight grip on Annie's hand. He talked and the others listened. He told the story of how his son's Grade 4 teacher—Miss Townsend—had told him and Annie in a parent-teacher conference that Taylor ought to see someone professionally for his panicked outbursts, but Mac thought that was tippy-toes city talk, like some real fucking weak-ass-woman-ass bullshit, and when they got back home he made Taylor sit at the kitchen table and write *I am not a fucking baby* over and

over and over and over and over and over and over and over
and and over and over and over and over and over and over
and again until his fingers blistered from holding the pencil,
and Taylor hadn't cried in front of him once since. That's
how real parenting is done, Mac said. Bet your kid Danny
can't handle shit without tears—not my Taylor.

Oh, Mac, Eliza said. Jameson did let you pick this year's
game, didn't he? You're his right hand, after all. Last year's
was thrilling. I felt so outside myself. You made me feel like
a new woman, Mac.

Annie snorted. Mac dug his nails hard into her palm.

Same game, he said, but a bigger prize for the winner. A
generous donation from the big man himself.

Eliza smiled.

But you won't go too hard on us, right, Mac?

Mac put his hands up in fake surrender.

I make no promises, he said.

Late into the night, after the food was eaten and the money
was raised and most of the guests had gone home, Mac
told the security guard he would see the remaining guests
out and lock up himself. Mac could convince people of
anything. Lucille Winston, Albert Riccio, Eliza, Lionel, and
Annie stayed behind.

After the group drank the bar dry, Mac led them all up a
staircase to the rooftop so the party could continue in the
open night air.

Lucille scanned the rooftop terrace until her eyes settled
on a large green electrical box in the far-left corner. She used
her kitten heels like grappling hooks to hoist herself up, then
splayed out on her back atop the green box like a starfish.

A metal ladder led from the terrace up to a higher platform with a large water heater. The Kilbers climbed up and sat cross-legged in front of the heater. They threw their wine glasses over the ledge and watched as they shattered onto Main Street below.

Albert removed his suit jacket and hung it over a ladder rung. He called up to the Kilbers, but they pretended they couldn't hear him.

At two in the morning, Mac called for everyone to quiet down. It was time for the game, he announced.

He told everyone that he would be It. No one disagreed.

Eliza cleared her throat with difficulty and said that she was a little too drunk to play. My Danny sleepwalks around three in the morning—I should be there when he's up. He could stumble out the front door into the street or break his neck tripping on the garden hose. I think I left it out after I watered the pelargoniums.

Mac said that if she didn't want to play, she shouldn't have agreed earlier. He stood in the centre of the terrace and covered his eyes with his hand. He began to count to ten.

Lucille, Albert, and Lionel scattered in different directions. Annie sprinted to the metal ladder. Her bundle of red curls came out of their French twist as she ran. When she was safely up on the water heater, she looked back at Eliza, who hadn't moved. She looked disoriented and overwhelmed, unsure of where to go.

Eliza began to stammer. Just let me go home and I'll come back. I promise I'll come back, Mac. You can trust me. Mac, I *swear*.

Eight. Seven.

Mac, please just let me see Danny—

Six. Five.

This is fucking insane, Mac, I can't do this—

Four. Three.

Mascara streaked down Eliza's face.

I'll do anything else, let me do anything else—

Two.

Please.

One.

Everyone froze where they were.

Mac stretched his arms out wide but kept his eyes closed. Eliza covered her mouth with her silk scarf to muffle her breathing. The others stayed as still as they could in their hiding places, trying to keep quiet. Mac spun around twice and started to walk with his arms out in front of him.

Lucille crawled across the top of the green electrical box, heels in hand, and slowly lowered herself back down onto the terrace.

Mac's head flicked up at the soft thud of Lucille's bare foot against the cement. His voice bellowed.

Grounders.

He opened his eyes and smiled down at her. She smiled back. She nodded. Annie shut her eyes.

Lucille placed her heels on top of her purse and little black beret. The wind blew up her dress as she walked to the edge of the rooftop. She stepped out as if to walk onto solid ground.

Then she was gone. Annie put her fist in her mouth and screamed.

Mac shut his eyes and counted to ten again.

Everyone shuffled and changed positions. When Mac got to one, Lionel stepped on his own foot trying to get up the ladder to the water heater and slipped off. He swore aloud.

Mac smiled. Grounders, Lionel. I'd know the sound of you anywhere, buddy.

Lionel laughed and shot his hands up with an exasperated sigh.

You sure got me quick, man!

Sure did.

Lionel turned back to face his wife.

Liza honey, he said. Can you tell Danny not to go near the marshes? Can you tell him that for me?

Eliza covered her mouth to suppress a sob. She nodded.

Mac rolled his eyes.

Lionel backed up to the opposite end of the rooftop, then sprinted. His body sped over the edge and through the night air.

The game went on. Albert's body got stuck between the ladder and the wall, and Mac heard him struggling to squeeze out. He left his things in a neat pile on the roof before jumping off.

Then Annie's foot slipped and hit the side of the water tank with a reverberating ring.

Everyone stopped.

She got grounders, Eliza yelled. Mac, she got grounders. I saw. I saw her.

Mac didn't move. His smile hardened into a firm line. Eliza waved her hands up and down.

Mac. I heard her. You have to call it. You have to call grounders.

Annie and Mac locked eyes. Her curls bounced in the night wind.

Grounders, he said quietly.

Eliza grabbed Annie from behind and pushed her off the water tank. Annie screamed. The bottom of her dress ripped.

Then she was at the edge. The open air bellowed. Annie put a hand over her mouth.

Go, Eliza shouted.

Give her a fucking second, Mac snapped.

Eliza backed away until it was just Mac and Annie.

She had expected Eliza to exclaim that the entire situation was ridiculous. She prayed that anyone would come to help her. No one did.

Mac did not rush her. He flicked his wrist back and forth and watched a little flash of light bounce off his cufflink from the moonlight.

I can't, Mac—I, I can't—

Here, Mac said, grabbing her wrists. I'll jump with you.

Eliza scoffed. What a fucking joke, she muttered. Annie's eyes widened.

But—but Taylor—

We're all that matters, he interrupted.

Annie could see the dazzling street lights. The bodies below slumped like stacked mattresses.

Mac smiled. He pulled the back of her head forward and stuck his tongue down her throat. She kept her face against his while she spun the two of them around. His silhouette against the lights below made it look as though a halo surrounded his body.

Annie broke away from Mac and pushed him backwards.

She saw the fear on his face as he fell. She wiped her mouth with the sleeve of her black dress and watched his head slam against the sidewalk and crack wide open.

When Annie turned around, Eliza was already gone.

Annie smoothed out her jacket and sat on the ledge in the cool night air, relishing a moment in which her time was her own. She heard quiet for the very first time.

It wasn't long before the beavers were on the bodies. One beaver stood upright on its hind legs with crimson on the fur of its nose and lips. It licked at the red of Mac's skull over and over and over and over and

I CAN OUTRUN YOU, TOO!

When Jacob Jameson climbed out of his bedroom window, the beaver was waiting for him in the backyard.

Thick fluffy fur covered its pudgy skin. Its whiskers were white, clean, and straight like a housecat's. Its front teeth moved slightly with its breath, rising and falling over its little chin. Tiny eyes scanned the backyard and its ears flicked back and forth. It stood up on its hind legs and watched Jacob calmly.

Jacob sat down cross-legged in the grass, soaking his PJ pants with dew. He asked the beaver if it had ever heard the song "Barges." Do you sing to one another when you go to sleep? Can you even hear songs underwater?

The beaver scratched its nose, then spoke:

What's a barge?

They're boats, Jacob said, but we have songs about other things, too. Like "Johnny Cake." Do you know "Johnny Cake"?

The beaver shook its head.

Jacob cleared his throat.

Johnny Cake ho, and Johnny Cake high, no one can catch me as I roll by. He's a cake that rolls out of the oven and the baker says *You can't run away Johnny Cake* and then Johnny Cake says *I've outrun an old man, a little girl, and I can outrun you, too* and then he rolls off through the town!

Jacob paused.

I should go back now. Will you be back tomorrow? I can teach you the song.

The beaver nodded.

Jacob climbed back through his window and rolled the muddy bottoms of his PJ pants up to his knees. He dreamt of cakes with thick fur, floating in the water of the marshes.

The only good thing about Jacob's childhood was the "Johnny Cake" song. He remembered listening to it on his father's Walkman—foam headphones twisted behind and over the tops of his ears. He liked how the narrator sounded as if he knew a secret the listener would never know. Jacob incessantly rewound the tape back to the "Johnny Cake" song. He wanted to know the secret.

> *I've outrun an old man, an old woman, a cow,*
> *a horse, and I can outrun you, too!*

The Pump smelled of rotting water. The Jamesons could never afford the houses on the cliffside, so they moved back and forth between apartment buildings near the marshes. Once, they stayed in one long enough for Jacob to paint his room—lime green on three walls and fire engine red on the fourth.

After his parents went to bed, Jacob would climb through his window into the backyard. The beaver was always there waiting for him. He would line his stuffed animals up against the fence alongside the beaver and play Prime Minister. He liked the idea that someone got to decide what everybody else should do, and he knew with certainty that he was good at making decisions. For starters, he never would've decided to move to The Pump.

He explained to the stuffed animals that only people born in The Pump should have to live there, nobody else, and only people with the name Jacob should get to see the beavers. Instead the beavers come up to every stupid family who goes to the marshes and it isn't fair because sometimes you want to feel special, sometimes you just want a friend who is a beaver all to yourself, but when your dad is paying to live inside another person's house you don't get anything all to yourself.

He wrote this speech out in crayon on the ripped cardboard back of a Quaker Oats box.

In the fall, a rusty telephone pole snapped at its base and smashed through the building's pipes. Their basement apartment flooded, and Jacob saw the cardboard piece with his speech shovelled up with the rest of the damp sewage into a pile in the living room. His mother blamed the accident on the beavers. The next time Jacob snuck out to meet his beaver, it never arrived.

The rest of it all felt less concrete—grey as the sky backdropping the stone lighthouse at the cove.

Jacob's mother had moved back home to Michigan; Jacob and his father stayed in The Pump. After seventeen years of raw-throated screaming between them, Jacob still chose to go to the university only a half-hour drive away so he could live at home while he studied. He made a few friends—ones he'd already sort of known in elementary and high school—but no new ones.

He met Mary Jameson in a Statistics of Business tutorial and for a month he accused her of lying about her name because there was *no way in hell* Jacob was going to have the same last name as someone he wasn't even related to. Her father owned the steel company Jameson Inc. and her mother ran a sesame-seed-bread business, which did extraordinary well down in the States. When he should've been studying, Jacob thought about Mary's square jaw and perfect bushy eyebrows. He graduated, but just barely.

They married soon after. The ceremony was held in the pumphouse rental hall. It was paid for with bread and steel money. Jacob spent his last half-hour before the wedding receiving his father's vicious insults. You're selling us out, Jake—you're a sellout. Sold your soul to fucking steelmakers.

Mary wore the green ball gown from her senior prom because it was the only thing she owned that was big enough to hide the baby bump. It rained as it did on most days in The Pump. Jacob's shoes sunk into the muddy moss and as he and Mary made their way onto the concrete boardwalk. His vows bled through the napkin he'd written them on, and he stumbled through a new speech on the spot, interrupted by his own frequent coughing.

Mary liked how she didn't even have to change her ID.

They got a house in the suburbs from Jameson Inc.—mortgage paid, more lawn than Jacob knew what to do with. Mary had to show him how the dishwasher worked. He covered it in vintage magnets, and she told him that he couldn't have all his stuff out when her parents came over for dinner.

When Mary went into labour, the Pump hospital had no rooms available. Case was born in Jacob's car in the parking lot of the *Daily Dam*, twenty or so feet from the hospital loading dock. Case shrieked and squirmed whenever Jacob held his pudgy body—banged his tiny fists against his plastic high-chair tray when Mary left for the office.

The only thing Jacob could ever do to calm Case down was to recite him the "Johnny Cake" song word for word. They both seemed to like the idea of a warm, round cake tricking stupid townspeople as it made its escape to freedom.

> *I outran an old man, and old woman, and I*
> *can outrun you, too!*

Soon it was just the three of them. First, Mary's parents (both in their eighties), who left ownership of the companies to her. Then Jacob's father—a hunting accident in the marshes.

Their deaths were quick; Mary went slowly. Stomach aches and dry patches at the back of her throat. Perpetual thirst. She started waking Jacob up in the middle of the night to tell him Case was a changeling—that he was an imposter child sleeping in her son's bed. That the storks had told her so. Jacob said they would move—sell the companies and go to Toronto, where they could at least go to a fucking Hudson's Bay Company to get Case a proper coat.

He found her body with her mouth agape, as if she had been surprised to go.

Jacob spent the years following on autopilot. He inherited his father-in-law's company that seemed like it was named for him. He signed cheques. He bought sports cars and old art and the silence of those he trusted most. He sent

Case to study abroad and to resort vacations and to sleep-away camp in the Kawarthas.

When Case was ten years old, Jacob caught him playing in a pocket of bog connected to the cove in the dead of night, lit only by the constellations above him. Case jumped off the mossy stones into the soupy mud, shrieking with joy—algae in his tumbled curls. He sprinted across the damp rocks, his voice raw from screaming, spat out green water, and repeated the ends of his own chants as if he had an echo:

> *I've outrun an old man and I can outrun you, too!*

> *And I can outrun you, too!*

> *I can outrun you, too!*

Jacob dragged Case home in his dripping clothes and gave him a choice of punishment: writing out the entire dictionary or getting the belt. Case sat in silence on the twin bed in his attic room while Jacob awkwardly rummaged through his closet to see if he even owned a belt. He ended up hitting Case's palms twice each with a wooden bookmark he found at the bottom of his desk drawer. Jacob looked at him and cried and said he just wanted to keep him from getting sick like how Mary got sick. Case pressed his palms against the cold metal of his bed frame and stayed silent.

Jacob did not want to be mayor, but he wanted to give Case what he wanted, and Case wanted the whole world. He skipped French class one morning and submitted his father's name for the nomination—then sat him down and planned him a speech of epic proportions for the campaign.

You need to talk about the beavers. That's what people want to hear about. Tell them they can hunt them—just during winter—but that it'll be the first thing you'll make official when you get in there. In office. They want jobs—they want to sell the pelts and make soft-as-fuck hats for the people in Richmond Hill—for rich people. They want to be the rich people. Tell them that you'll let them hunt the beavers and you'll be promising to make them the rich people.

It was an easy win. Jacob pawed at his dark curls and smiled with his teeth in every interview. He smiled and lied and dabbed sweat off his forehead with a handkerchief.

No one who mattered could catch the beavers. No fancy hats were made. None were sold. There were no rich people in The Pump—other than the Jamesons.

Case made the two of them go to a tailor in Niagara Falls to get fitted suits. He fought with the tailor himself who said he wouldn't make one in bright green. What, green isn't masculine enough? You don't think I can kick your ass in a green?

Jacob leaned against the counter and said nothing. Sometimes he was thankful to let Case do all the talking; sometimes he wasn't.

Jacob had never been one for words, let alone eloquent ones. Case knew what made people tick, but he wasn't the best at interacting with them. Case wrote and Jacob spoke. Their lives became a project of collaborative puppetry.

After three years, their system broke down. Jacob liked the administration aspect of the job, but Case started to care about *things*: the school curriculum, the environmental impact of Jameson Inc.'s industrial buildings, the unfinished and underfunded construction projects strewn around The Pump.

One night, the two of them stayed at the office till 4:30 a.m. Case threatened to show up to the next council meeting and tell the committee members about the dead Boy Scout, Maxi Miller. Jacob chose to block the whole thing out, as he did most things. A kid had died, but it wasn't *his* kid. Case was different than Jacob. Case cared about things that were not his.

There's nothing in any of these reports about the beavers, Case said.

They're being fed, Jacob said.

I'm *aware*.

Jacob sighed and bunched his hands into his curls.

It's just not a priority right now, he said.

Case swiped a pile of papers off the desk with his arm. Jacob's metal nameplate clattered to the floor at Case's shoes.

Fuck you, Case said. Fuck your priorities.

The next morning, nervous sweat wet Jacob's shirt as he typed an anonymous email and sent it to two addresses: the *Daily Dam* and the *Toronto Star*. Something about money should work, he thought. The headline hit both papers the next morning, and the Pump police showed up at the office by the afternoon.

> *Speechwriter and Son of Mayor Jacob Jameson Jailed for Embezzlement*

Case called his father's cellphone from the jailhouse. Jacob did not pick up. It vibrated against his wooden desk and moved in little semicircles. The guilt boiled deep in Jacob's bones. He started to cough again, wild and violent. The coughing turned to sobbing.

His secretary popped her head through his office door. We're set up—are we ready to go? He opened his mouth to speak, but nothing came out. He nodded.

His assistant slipped into his office. Yellow hair grazed her shoulders. She had sunken wrists and tired cheeks—teeth a little big for her mouth.

She passed him her speech, written on a café napkin. Jacob liked how Case had always typed up his speeches real nice on glossy white paper, letters in bold so he could see them better.

It would have to do.

At the press conference, Jacob told reporters that the people living in the houses near the marshes were lying. He explained that the lower class were mad about there not being enough beavers to hunt, and they were mad about not getting rich, so they were killing each other and blaming it on something that wasn't even there anymore. He told them that they were killing each other because they were poor—because they wished that they weren't from The Pump, but they were, and now they didn't want to exist.

He lied and told them that there was nothing wrong with the water—nothing wrong with the beavers. Trust me, he promised.

When Jacob Jameson shut off the office lights and turned to grab his briefcase, he found a beaver sitting on top of it.

He was sure he hadn't left the door or any windows open—hadn't heard the scamper of clawed feet against the hardwood floor. He blinked. The room appeared blurred through his tired eyes.

The beaver was still there, its leathery tail draped over the suitcase handle. Jacob eyed it carefully. His voice was hushed.

I lied for you, Jacob said.

The beaver stared back at him.

Jacob continued.

I could take you home. I could take you home and roast you in my oven. I could make a hat out of you. It's snowing. I could wear you out in the snow and my head would be warm and you wouldn't eat anyone ever again.

The beaver raised a paw to its tiny mouth and coughed. Its voice was low and raspy.

I can outrun you, too, it said.

DANNY BOY

You only buy the blue popsicles from Mr. Arbour at Eggs & Things after somebody dies. They cost five ninety-nine each. There's a lump of red dye in the middle, and after you finish the whole thing, you stick the stick to the side of someone's plastic recycling bin.

The people who have died are usually acquaintances, which lets you enjoy the popsicle without feeling guilty for having a moment of happiness.

The day Danny Kilber dies, your popsicle tastes rancid. When it melts under your tongue, it feels sticky and sweaty, like it doesn't belong in your mouth at all. You drop it half-eaten in the dead grass outside the store. You crouch down and watch it melt and dye the ants red and blue, as if they're playing flag football.

Everyone talks about Danny Kilber's death. They say that his eardrums splattered against the tracks behind Mr. Desperate's bar before he even heard the train. There was nothing left for the coroner. They say it happened because Danny was stupid enough to wear two-hundred-dollar noise-cancelling headphones. They say he tried to cut across town so he wouldn't be late for his shift at the gallery. It's a solid shift: four to nine every Wednesday and Saturday for just shy of twelve dollars an hour. When you are asked if you want his job—three days after the funeral—you gladly accept.

You figure it's a gift from Danny: something to make up for the two years he never got you a birthday present. You always got him something good. You bought him those noise-cancelling headphones. The train hit him a month after the warranty ended. Part of you wishes Danny would've been dumb enough to get himself killed in June instead of July so you could've gotten your money back. He died in his uniform, so you have to buy your own.

You're late on your first day. Your boss watches porn in the back office while you scrub dirt marks off the white gallery walls with a Magic Eraser. The phone rings every twenty minutes or so. You assure a caller that his daughter won't be exposed to grass during art camp next week, although you don't really know for sure if that's true.

The gallery show hasn't been rotated since before you were born. You remember when you visited Danny at work once and the two of you sat with your backs pressed against one of the storage room's cold white walls, sharing potato soup. You covered your mouth to muffle the sound of your laughing while he gave the paintings new names. He pointed to realistic sketches of cliffs and named them *Drowning Labia* and *Banana and Pear #46*. He once named a painting after the contents of an entire grocery receipt, with the taxes and the little survey at the bottom for your chance to win a gift card and everything. He used to say that art only existed to make people like him feel bad about not being able to make art. You told him that he could draw well enough, even though you both knew that he couldn't.

All the paintings in the gallery are of the lighthouse on the cove at the edge of town. Its dull stone spire look the same to every artist, as if no one on earth can see it any other way than how it is meant to be seen. Each piece is a collage of grey and dark green. Other colours do not exist in The Pump.

Girls come in to look at the art. One of them is probably your future wife. You know you'll never leave here. You're rooted deep in the damp Pump ground.

Every one of them smells like fake orange rinds and moth balls. Each Pump girl has little dark round Pump eyes that can see through the thick morning fog and can tell if you'll cheat on her or not.

The only girl to come in on your first day has long black hair pulled back into a bad French braid. She stands in front of the painting *Lighthouse at Dawn*. You watch as she snaps off a grey corner of the canvas, shoves it into her mouth, and swallows. She looks around, then speeds into the next room.

You aren't sure if your boss would get mad if he found out that you didn't intervene while someone ate a painting. You hide behind the raised edge of the doorframe and peer into the next gallery. The girl is the only one in the room. She stands in front of *Lighthouse in Mid-Spring*, scrapes some paint off the green water with her fingernails, and sucks the chips off her fingers like one of your blue popsicles.

Danny would've said something. He would've asked her what she was doing in a way that didn't make her feel ashamed. You just watch.

At *Lighthouse: A Study* in the hallway connecting the galleries, the girl sniffs around the frame like an anteater before licking a patch of dark on the canvas. She grimaces and draws back, as if she can taste Lake Ontario in all its grimy truth.

Your shoulder hits the wooden door frame and her eyes dart to where you're standing. She acts as if you've witnessed something she wanted you to see. Her parting lips reveal a crowd of large teeth.

You're Daniel Kilber's friend.

You nod. You ask how she knows him.

She says that Danny used to let her come in and taste the paintings whenever she wanted. You cool with that? You have his job now, don't you?

You don't tell her the job is all you have left of Danny. You don't tell her that since he died, you see sunrises and they don't make you feel a thing. It's like you radiate numbness outward until your body feels like it's standing still but across the room; like you're everywhere and nowhere all at once; like you're filling entire parks and bank entrances and intersections with your numbness. You don't tell her that you feel perpetually seasick from existing in a place Danny no longer inhabits. That breathing makes you nauseous. That you've stopped dreaming while you sleep. That you read and watch a lot of things about how you're supposed to feel a dead person's presence around you like a ghost or guardian angel and that you still don't feel anything. That you name paintings after what they look like. That you do not want to exist in a world without your best friend.

Can't really risk my job for someone I don't know. It pays well. Sorry.

She smiles at you. More teeth. Green flecks.

I knew Daniel well. Really well. We can work something out.

We really can't.

Do you want to talk to him?

You huff angrily. She's wasting your time. You're going to get fired and it'll be this Pump girl's fault. But you ask what she's talking about anyway.

She asks you again if you'd like to talk to Danny.

You nod before you even realize you're doing it. Your desperation to see your best friend overcomes your doubt.

She tells you she'd like to make a deal: on Wednesdays, you let her come into the gallery and taste all the paintings she wants and in exchange she writes you a letter once a week—a letter from Danny.

Her proposal is the stupidest idea that you've ever heard in your entire life.

You agree.

On Wednesday, the first letter is waiting on your desk. The girl smiles at you with her large teeth and waves from her place in Gallery One. You rip the letter open without finesse:

Dear Milo,

> *I think I miss you, or whatever. When I picture your stupid hair it makes me nervous in a good way, which I think is what missing someone is? I had a dream the other night that me and you and George Bush Sr. built a raft out of chemistry textbooks to escape an apocalyptic flood. I don't think I've had a dream in the last ten years without you in it. It's stupid really.*

> *I broke your Nirvana CD today. I brought it to that psych-ward summer camp, so I'd have something to listen to, but then I remembered that I hate Nirvana, because they're really shitty. Do people even use CDs anymore? I'll buy you a new one if they still make them. If*

not, I'll just record the sound of tin foil in the microwave for you. It'll sound about the same.

The marshes should be our new spot. Like, OUR spot. Better than that construction development anyway. Less nails. Remember when we'd camp there for Boy Scouts? I guess they call it Beavers now. Funny.

Read these letters while drinking Orange Crush. The words'll taste better.

—D

You find the girl after your shift, your fingers tightly clutching the damp envelope. You shove the letter in her face.

How did you know all this? About him?

I told you. Danny and I were—

Close, yeah, you said that. That's bullshit. I would've known you if you were that close.

You don't want the letter? No problem. I'll take it back.

She tightens her fingers around the envelope but you don't loosen your grip. The two of you lock eyes. She burps—white canvas dust on her lips and turpentine on her breath.

See you next Wednesday.

You reread the letter twice a day every day. You know it's not real but you need it anyway. You can hear his stupid exaggerated sneeze and see the muddy footprints of his size-ten shoes on the hardwood of your dining room floor. You spend your entire first paycheque on Orange Crush.

The gallery is crowded the next Wednesday. All the retired couples in town come at nine in the morning to see

Lighthouse Observed come out of the archives to go up in Gallery Two. You serve them one-year-old white wine and brie cheese with flax seeds in it. Everyone accidently wears salmon. Every Pump woman pins a flower brooch onto her cardigan. Mrs. Miller's is a pelargonium filled with purple amethyst stones.

You don't see the girl at the opening, but when you get back to your desk for your break, a second letter is there.

Dear Milo,

I saw your mom at the Bridal Shop the other day buying three or four issues of National Geographic. *She looked tired. I think all girls just look tired though. Staying alive as a girl seems like it's a full-time job.*

I've been dreaming about the marshes. I feel like we're supposed to do something there. I feel like I forgot something in the mud that I need to go back and find, but I don't know what it is. Not something physical—like, a feeling maybe. Like a part of myself. Bullshit, I know. Whatever. I hope you understand what I'm talking about.

Does Jenny Carpenter still work at the the Rag & Bean Coffee Co.? She never put enough sugar in anything. Every coffee I ever got from her was disappointing. Not like, your-mother-not-surviving-a-car-crash disappointing, but like, you booked a hotel room for a trip with the family, and you

*packed the car with your shit, like packed,
like each person can't even move an arm and
is holding bags on their laps, and you drive
hours to the hotel to find that administration fucked up, and somebody else is in your
room, and you can't get another one because
there aren't any extra, and you can't sleep in
the car because it's so jam-packed, so you're
driving around in your jam-packed car at
two-thirty in the morning, and you're in a
really remote part of the city and there aren't
any twenty-four-hour McDonald's around,
only the ones that close at, like, eleven on a
Friday, and your wife is screaming at Siri to
find a goddamn cheap motel nearby and Siri
keeps responding by linking you to the lyrics
for "Hotel California," and you're sitting in
the driver's seat, watching your left headlight
flicker in and out, wondering if anyone else
in the universe could possibly feel this disap-
pointed.*

I hope you're getting some ass.

—D

When you lock up, you notice that *Lighthouse Observed* is
slightly popped out of its frame. The pine trees in the painting's left corner are torn, as if the world's smallest chainsaw
had eaten through them.

You start to enjoy waking up in The Pump. You write responses to Danny's letters and throw them over the cove's cliffs into the lake, as if the storks will tell Danny what you have to say. You think more about the marshes than you ever have before: the smell of the moss, the squish of the mud beneath flat dark rocks, the beavers. You like to block things out, but now they all flood back in, and you aren't afraid or guilty or sad—you're restless. You wonder if the girl ever went to the marshes with Danny.

When you arrive in the morning to unlock the gallery, she's standing at the front door. Her black hair is every-where at once, covering her face and arms. She asks if you slept well. The glint of sunlight makes her teeth look even bigger.

You ask her for the letter. It's Wednesday. The letter? It's Wednesday, you know? Did you forget? Did you forget the letter?

She smiles and hands you a ripped piece of notebook paper from her jacket pocket, folded in half, no envelope. She walks back down the street without even going into the gallery.

You throw your coat onto the gallery floor before heading to your desk. The paper is damp—almost wet.

Dear Milo,

I left them for you in the marshes.

—D

You flip the OPEN sign to CLOSED against the window of the gallery.

The bog water swarms with horseflies. You get bitten twice on your walk through the marshes. The bites aren't raised bumps—they're pink concaves where chunks of skin have been ripped out. Nettle stings your ankles and burrs latch to the ankles of your jeans.

The girl is waiting for you. Her sweater and jeans are laid out in the mud, slowly sinking. She stands in the dark green water in nothing but her bra and underwear. Her long hair frizzes and curls down past the nape of her neck.

You tell her you've read the letter. That you know that Danny left something here just for you.

She says you're right—there is something here for you. She has something to give you.

She unhooks her bra. It falls away into the mud. She lifts each leg out of the water, then throws her underwear behind her. She stands naked in front of you. For a moment, you wonder if this is what Danny wanted you to have. You step into the water, fully clothed, and walk toward her. Your hands are on her bare shoulders, her back, in her hair, across her chest. Your mouth is full of her teeth and tongue.

Her arms shorten against your body; her neck broadens and sinks below her shoulder blades; her face juts farther out than it ever did before; her skin is covered in thick fur. The bottom of her spine breaks through skin and flattens into a large, heavy tail. She flaps it against the water. Once. Twice.

You taste blood in your mouth and break off to look at her. She is a thing of nightmares, but you cannot stop yourself from touching her face. You cannot stop smiling. A laugh bursts up from your gut. Her beady eyes narrow.

What? What's funny?

Her voice is clear and calm. She lets go of your hands.

Why—why are you looking at me like that?

She stumbles backward. She looks up at you in fear. What the—holy fuck holy *fuck*.

You reach up to touch your own face and feel a handful of lush fur. Your clothes have ripped and fallen away. They float in soaked shards around your thick legs. Long dark nails replace your own.

The two of you are matching monstrosities.

You smell things you've never been able to smell before—a putrid reek in the air. The human you falls away. You are not afraid; you are relieved.

The two of you explore one another. Her whiskers twitch.

She dives into the water first, beckoning you to follow.

You thrust forward.

The two of you swim. Neither of you feels the need to speak. You no longer need words. You will not use them where you are headed.

LIFE GIVER

Wren decided that he was going to marry a nurse. Nurses made good wives. His nurse-wife would have lots of work-related things to talk about but not so much as to overwhelm him with her chatter. Nurses really knew their shit, like all the shit you would need to know to be a wife and a nurse. Wren didn't know his shit at all—any of it. He wanted someone to know his shit for him. That was what wives were for.

Rochelle was his Almost Girl. She was an intern at the little hospital in the centre of town, which made her almost a nurse, and they had kissed once in the triage parking lot after she showed Wren how to calm his bloody nose, which made her almost his girl. Her curly red hair made her almost pretty.

For their first date, Rochelle took him to Mr. Desperate's for a beer. Green paint peeled off the wooden booth seats. Ragged cotton fluff peeked out from the cushions. Half the light bulbs were dead. Old, half-ripped flyers were plastered on the bulletin board near the front door. One with a picture of a bird bore the text LOST PARAKEET. GOES BY THE NAME OF HONEY. $15 REWARD. Rochelle ordered for the two of them, then poured out sugar packets onto the table and lined up the crystals as if she were doing coke. She said she wanted to freak out the server. She liked freaking people out. She asked Wren if he was freaked out. He choked on his beer.

Do you want me to be?

Honest answer.

A little? Not really. Just a bit.

Freaked out like you want to leave?

Um, no?

She pinched the pile of sugar with her fingertips and put it on her tongue. It dissolved like snowflakes.

I have a secret.

Wren blinked.

Okay?

I can't tell you though. It's pretty bad. You'd probably throw up if I told you—throw up and tell me to fuck off. Maybe even kill yourself.

Wren put down his beer and lowered his voice to a whisper.

Did you…murder someone?

Rochelle shook her head.

Wren kind of *did* want to tell her to fuck off. She leaned in close with her elbows splayed out on the tabletop.

I told you—I can't tell you what it is.

She flopped back into her seat and didn't mention the secret for the rest of the night. She ordered two more beers and talked about how old Paul McCartney was getting and how big epidural needles were and how one time when she was ten she spilled apple juice on her dad's tax papers and he beat the shit out of her with an extension cord. Wren knew that Rochelle was only trying to get him to ask about the secret. He kind of liked how manipulative that was.

He also liked how she was bossy. He laid awake in bed after the date thinking about how she'd tell him to pick up the clothes in his disgusting room but also how she'd probably put on every single one of his shirts just to freak him out.

He heard scratching at the door, but when he went to investigate, there was nothing there. He returned to bed. He drifted off into dreams so wild that they could only have been constructed by Rochelle.

She talked about the secret a lot but never directly. She liked to call Wren on her break and tell him how excited he was going to be when she finally told him. I'm gonna fuck your world view so hard you'll give birth to my ideas, she'd say. I'm gonna blow your mind into bits, little boy.

Wren kept changing the subject. He'd ask if she'd watched Jacob Jameson talk about the water on the Q101 local news. He'd say that he dropped his phone in his bowl of cereal and needed to put it in rice to suck all the milk out. It was hard to get her to stop talking about the secret. It was even harder to stop thinking about it.

They had sex on his apartment building's laundry room floor and he told her that he thought he might love her. She picked bits of dryer lint from her thighs and told him that he wouldn't love her when he knew the truth. I promise, he said, I won't care. I won't care what you did. If you just tell me I swear I won't care—not at all. I'll care less than nothing.

She smiled.

Fine, then. Let's shower.

Wren startled. Showering wasn't something you did for fun in The Pump—you showered when you ran out of bottled water to boil on the stovetop. He couldn't remember the last time he'd intentionally let water from the pipes hit his body. Everything smelled like the lake.

But Rochelle was the kind of girl who made you want to do things you normally didn't want to do.

The two of them stood in his grimy porcelain tub. Rochelle leaned over and pulled out a travel-sized shampoo container from her bag on the bathroom floor.

I want you to trust me. I like you a fuck ton and I want you to trust me.

Wren nodded. He didn't have any particularly strong feelings toward the act of shampooing one's hair. He moved the shower head to the right so that the water would stop hitting their bodies.

Rochelle squeezed the bottle and tipped it upside down above her palm.

Blood came out.

It felt like watching a movie. Wren didn't speak. He watched her dump the contents of the bottle on top of her head.

He had never seen her look so beautiful. Her hair was slicked back and flushed crimson, little red droplets running down her temples like tears. She let the cold blood drip through her dark curls and over the tops of her ears. The room reeked like pennies. She rubbed it into her skin until she was satisfied, then turned the shower head back toward her to wash it off. It was like watching a baptism.

Slowly she poured out a little bit more from the bottle and took Wren's hand in her own. He jerked to move away, but she held her grip and pressed the blood into his hand. He relaxed. She rubbed the blood up into the skin of his arm.

The two of them stood in the tub looking like they had come out of a massacre. Wren couldn't stop staring at his fingernails. Rochelle softly gripped his chin.

This is helping you. Trust me.

She kissed him. The metallic taste was horrendous in his mouth, but he wanted to enjoy the sensation of her lips on his. He didn't pull away. He wanted to have babies with Rochelle. He wanted their babies to have thick hair and two normal eyes and he didn't want them to smell like Pump water.

Rochelle asked what the scratching sound was. Wren poked his head out of the curtain. He could hear it, faintly, but couldn't decipher where in the house it was coming from. Must be tree branches hitting the siding, he figured.

After, they lay on the couch wrapped in their towels and Rochelle explained that the blood kept her from getting sick. It keeps me safe, she said. But it's gotta be from someone who wasn't born here. Our blood's too fucked up from—well, you know. I can't explain the science, but you just gotta go for it. Here, take mine. Try on a little, like a moisturizer, like you'd use coconut oil before you go to bed. You can wash your hands from the tap and everything. It's like a shield. I feel wholly new, I swear, Wren. It's like a cleanse.

She filled empty bottles with the emergency stock inside the surgery theatres. She talked her way into getting every twenty-four-hour shift she needed so that she would be the only intern on the entire floor. He liked that she could talk anybody into doing anything she wanted.

He tried washing his hands with it that night—scrubbed the pale spots on his skin raw until it looked like he'd been fingerpainting. He only smelled the metallic scent of the blood—no lake water. No burning. No sores on his knuckles the morning after.

The first time she let him come along on her weekly heist, his body was wracked with an energy that made him want to skip down the halls. Both of their bags were filled with shampoo bottles. On their way down in the elevator to the main entrance, Wren found himself looking at a poster for blood donation that was plastered above the buttons. A lady with a turquoise blouse and too-wide smile sat on a love seat next to an older man with one eye and one leg. They were connected by a red ribbon at their wrists that came together at the centre in a big bow. Above them in bold script were the words THE POWER OF JESUS CHRIST RUNS THROUGH YOUR VEINS. BE A LIFE GIVER. DONATE TODAY.

Almost immediately, Wren went from using the blood once a week to twice a day. Rochelle kept track of the out-of-town patients who were admitted and filled bottles until he had too many to stack on the metal shelf in his shower. He'd wait for her in the hospital parking lot an hour before her shift ended because his body couldn't physically be away from her any longer.

They got beer at Mr. Desperate's every Wednesday night. She talked about her day while Wren watched her in awe and occasionally nodded. She raved about how she got called as backup for the paramedics on the ambulance because a kid got hit by a train. There was nothing left of him to clean up, left alone to treat, she explained.

He just nodded, sipped at his beer. He thought about the blood at random points throughout the day, mostly when he missed Rochelle.

It was harder for her to get enough blood for the both of them. During an ice storm, the Red Cross in Toronto called and said their truck wouldn't be coming south for at least a week. The hospital's theatre was full of blood from local patients, but idiots from the city rarely came to The

Pump for medical care. Rochelle came to Wren empty-handed two Wednesdays in a row. Wren didn't shower for the full two weeks.

One day, after pacing his apartment, he decided to walk down to the hospital to bring Rochelle lunch. He found her on the fifth floor, wiggling a broken hairpin into the slot of the vending machine. Purple bloomed below his bloodshot eyes. He let her talk about her morning until his brain pulsed against his skull, then interrupted her to ask if she had any extra blood. I just need a little to get me through until after the trucks come back. Just a little bit, just a cap full.

Rochelle snorted and shoved the pin entirely into the coin slot. She kicked the machine until a bag of trail mix fell to the bottom. She picked out the mouldy peanuts and threw them in the closet recycling bin. Don't have any for you.

He looked at her as if he didn't recognize her. He clutched the sandwich he'd brought for her so hard that it squished in his fist like a stress ball.

Rochelle—you're kidding me, right? This is a joke?

She drew her body closer until their noses almost touched. She smiled.

If you really love me, you'll wait.

She walked away. He half-jogged to the elevator so he could go down to the cafeteria. His heartbeat bellowed in his ears. He swore he could feel his blood sloshing around beneath his skin. The lady from the BE A LIFE GIVER poster smiled above him like she was anointing him.

He left the elevator and went to sit in the ER waiting room on the third floor. A teenage girl with long blond curls slumped in a chair, picking at a large purple scab on her cheek. An older woman sat beside her, smoothing her hair and whispering softly. Just shut them out, Margaret. Just shut the words out.

A woman with loud shoes bumped into Wren as he was standing up to stretch. Her scorching coffee poured over the green tile floor. She apologized, then asked Wren if he worked in the hospital.

He mopped the coffee up with an old *Hello!* magazine and lied about how many patients he'd saved as a cardiovascular surgeon, because it seemed like something Rochelle would do. She explained that her father was dying upstairs. Thank the Good Lord finally—I mean, I drove all the way here in that shitshow outside twice last week 'cause he *claimed* he was kicking the bucket, but he had the nerve to stay a couple more days. I mean, I love him and all, but it's really his time. He deserves a break from himself. We *all* deserve a break.

She said her name was Kelly Johnson. She asked Wren what there was to do in The Pump. My kids are fine upstairs praying or whatever the fuck. I'm not gonna keep walking laps and hoping I get some deathly disease just by breathing hospital air.

Something in Wren wanted Kelly's blood more badly than he knew how to control. He spat out an answer without out a moment of contemplation:

Beaver hunting. You should go beaver hunting. Everyone down here does it.

He gave her the directions to the Fishing Co., where they sold oversized butterfly nets. Even kids hunt here. It's like catching bugs really. They walk right over to you like cats. You'll get enough in an hour to make yourself a nice hat— you know, for the shithole weather.

The sound of her heels echoed off the walls as she left through the automatic doors.

Wren sat back in a triage seat and closed his eyes. He had almost fallen asleep when he heard a voice behind him.

Are you a doctor?

Wren opened one eye. The blond girl was sitting by herself in the row across from him. She scratched her face.

Not really, he said.

Oh, she said.

Wren shut his eyes again, but the girl cleared her throat.

I'm probably gonna die, you know.

Wren sighed and sat up.

We're all going to die, he said.

I mean soon, the girl clarified.

She smiled. She pointed to the scab on her face.

Wren knew vaguely about the rash, though he deliberately turned the local news off when they mentioned it so as to keep a little peace of mind. He knew it had something to do with the water. He knew the people who got it were locals. Local blood couldn't cure anything.

You don't seem all that bummed about it, Wren said. About dying, I mean.

Everyone dies, she said, but not everyone gets to be a part of history. I caught something that's gonna be in books. My mother will sob at my funeral. She was so young, she'll say. The picture they use for the obituary will be me at peak beauty. The town might even name a street after me or something. Margaret Memorial Lane. Maybe people'll name babies after me.

This is what you'd choose? Wren asked. If you got to choose how you'd die, you'd pick this?

She shrugged.

It's interesting, isn't it?

I don't think I'd pick the most *interesting* thing, Wren said.

Then who will care? Margaret asked. If someone reads about your death, why would they be invested in it if you just died like everybody else?

Wren didn't know how to answer.

We're all from the same town, Margaret continued. And most of us die the same way.

She raised her hands up like claws and curled her bottom lip under her two front teeth.

The beavers, Wren said.

Exactly, Margaret said. It was a big deal back when Maxi Miller died but now we're like, numb. It happens so often that people are there and then they're just not. Sometimes we don't even know they're gone. Sometimes we didn't even know they were there in the first place.

Wren nodded.

Margaret continued.

I don't know you, Margaret said. I don't even know your name. If you got eaten tomorrow, I wouldn't know and most of the people in The Pump wouldn't know. They wouldn't care. I wouldn't care. We're used to it now, you see. Why would I care? Why should I?

Wren paused to think about it.

I don't know, he said.

When Kelly Johnson returned to the hospital a day later, her left hand was missing.

Dr. Flynn marked her file HUNTING ACCIDENT. Everyone knew what that meant. After she was cauterized and stitched clean like a doll, they put her bed in an empty storeroom on the second floor to make space for other patients. Rochelle tugged at Wren's hair as they rode up the elevator for her night shift. Her hot breath tickled the inside of his ear. Be a Life Giver.

Once they were in the room, they moved a metal cabinet to blockade the door. Wren bit off his fingernails while

Rochelle set up the needle and IV tube. He broke three pairs of gloves—she sighed and spilled half a bottle of antiseptic into his palms. His throat was dry. We're only taking a little. Just a little.

Just a little, she repeated.

Everything slowed down. The rain outside hit the glass of the window in intervals, like the fading beat of a drum. His feet almost gave way when Kelly's blood began to flow up the plastic tube and into the bag.

He thought about what it might be like to drown in that blood. To gasp for air as it flooded his space and soaked his clothes. To pound his fists into the plastic of the bag while his vision went dark and red. To feel it gurgle at the back of his throat. A symphony of cells pouring into his ears. Peace.

Rochelle hooked up a new bag. Then a third. A fourth. Wren couldn't stop looking at the door, waiting to be caught at any moment.

That's a little fucking more than a little.

She licked her lips—grabbed his wrist and put the IV in his hand.

Time to save yourself, little boy.

The heat of the bag pulsed through his fingers. The pumping of her blood almost felt like the echo of waves in a seashell. He closed his eyes. Held his breath.

A beeping brought him back to reality. The lines on the monitor above Kelly's bed began to stretch and touch the top and bottom of the screen. Rochelle packed the blood in a cooler filled with ice. Wren kept filling new bags.

The beeping quickened. Kelly's face greyed. Sweat rolled down Wren's hairline. A little more. A little more.

A little more.

A solid tone. Loud. Uninterrupted. Wren dropped the IV. Rochelle pooled the blood into her palms to save it from soaking into the sheets. Unplugged the monitor. Covered the body. Moved the cabinet out of the way.

Wren stood still. Rubbed his fingers together. The lines between his prints darkened. He didn't notice Rochelle's hand gripping his shoulder.

It's a hospital. People die every day.

She changed Kelly's file in the computer. BLED OUT DURING SURGERY. TIME OF DEATH—4:56. She drove them to his apartment.

Wren tried to wipe the blood off his hands. It streaked his pale shirt with bright handprints.

She filled a third of the tub with the blood. He sat cross-legged, silent, while she painted a lighthouse on his bare back with her fingers.

Later, she slept beside him in bed. She snored and cocooned herself in the dark blue sheets while Wren lay stiff as a board.

Then he heard the scratching.

He went into the living room. Rochelle's bloody lighthouse painting was still sticky on the skin of his back. The scratching stopped—then started again.

He opened the front door. Moonlight gleamed against his red-streaked face.

The beaver on his doorstep twitched its nose. Another poked its head out of a nearby bush. And another.

Wren tried to wipe the blood off his body. The first beaver stood up on its back legs and looked at Wren curiously as he struggled. It sniffed around his feet, nibbling dried blood on his toenail. Wren did not scream.

The beavers gorged.

MAL AUX DENTS
(OR TOOTHACHE)

I hadn't gotten my mouth looked at since my regular checkup last year when my dentist, Dr. Dan, walked out to log my patient data into the computer and dropped dead from a heart attack. I was already nervous to go 'cause I was convinced pretending I was straight had rotted my teeth out. A lie like that eats your insides. When Dr. Dan left the exam room, I didn't realize he was, like, dying, so I convinced myself that he walked out 'cause he knew and was going to tell all the dental hygiene students my dirty little secret.

He died in the other room, so I didn't hear anything—I'm not traumatized or whatever. I remember knowing for sure that I'd been in the Frankenstein chair for too long. When the paramedics arrived, they didn't even let me wash my mouth out with the little metal squirting thing. I stood in the parking lot in my socks with that bubble gum shit still smeared on my gums.

This time, one of my teeth had to be pulled. When the new dentist ripped the Swiss cheese molar out of my mouth, I asked if I could keep it. I rolled it around in my palm and inspected its little black dots while my mom gave her credit card info to the receptionist.

Mom and I walked down John Street toward the pump-house and she asked if I liked my new dentist. He's better than the fucking dead one, I thought. Well, yeah, I said. I knew she was only trying to get me talking 'cause she was worried that my dead dentist reminded me of my dead dad and she didn't want me to jump off an office building like he had. I answered her questions as we cut across the soccer field. Muddy water soaked through my Walmart sneakers.

We parted ways in the parking lot. She handed me a Thermos of chicken noodle soup and left to meet our neighbour, Mrs. Miller, for their Bible study.

Lachlan Reese greeted me at the door to the pump-house. His blond hair stuck up in tufts like the feathers of a baby duck. We were wearing the same green camp counsellor sweaters, but his seemed nicer, probably 'cause he wasn't a sinner. He smiled at me and I looked down at my wet sneakers.

Morning, Taylor! he yelled. How lucky we are to be alive today!

Um, yeah, I said. Yes. Uh, that's true. Yes. Good morning.

He reached forward to shake my hand even though he had already met me like fifty times. I didn't want to shake his hand so I waved instead and we both stood in awkward silence until I put my hands in my pockets and snuck past him into the gymnasium to grab my lanyard and name tag off the fold-out table.

Then I saw Laurent Bordeaux. He was sitting cross-legged on the gym floor wrapping pink yarn around popsicle sticks to make a cat's cradle for Milo Riccio's little brother, Emmett. Emmett had a sticky ring of apple juice around his mouth. The speaker was blaring the song "Our God Is an Awesome God." Everything smelled like sweat.

Laurent tied off the yarn and handed it to Emmett, who quickly threw it back and yelled that he couldn't have a pink one 'cause boys don't get pink ones. Laurent ran a hand through his dark hair and said that God loves all people, no matter what colours they like. Emmett stared back at him blankly like he didn't get it.

The Bordeauxs were the newest hot gossip 'cause they had just moved to The Pump from Montreal. Anyone who spoke differently from the majority of us was interesting enough to be talked about at the Home Hardware check-out. I didn't really care 'cause my mom was French, so none of it was new to me.

Nothing ruins you like having a French mother. The French get all riled up and passionate about things, and they always sound like they're saying something about sex when they're really just talking about the weather, and they're all objec-tively beautiful like my mom, Annie. I used *I have a French mom* as the interesting fact about myself when the teacher went around the table to do introductions on the first day of CALC 101. That was the real obnoxious part—how often I felt the need to tell other people about my French mother, as if it made me more worldly or something. I couldn't even speak French 'cause when I came around, my mom was too busy trying to learn English. I wasn't even French enough to be half French. All I was good at was being a bridge, like when I had to explain to my mom that a pipe cleaner wasn't a person, or that people wouldn't know what she was talking about if she told them to *close the light*. I knew less French than people who weren't even French. It made me feel fake.

Laurent was way more French than me—he even had a fucking French name. I guess God wanted both of us to be church camp leaders for the summer, so there we were. I swerved through the plastic chairs and walked right up to him like I wasn't completely petrified to make human contact. I had worked everything out the night before. I was gonna go, *Hey, you're Laurent!* or maybe even a confident *Hey, Laurent* or *Hey, dude.* I was gonna be like, *Yo, Laurent, dude. Bro. Nice cat's cradles. You have some great technique,* which I figured was much better than saying he had great fingers, even though his cuticles were fucking flawless.

I went up to him and he looked at me and he smiled and I forgot who the fuck I was or what I was doing there. Then he started talking first, which I totally wasn't prepared for.

Hi. You're Taylor, right?

He looked down at my name tag.

Tay. Sorry, I knew that. Do you want me to call you Tay? It says Tay on your name card, but I don't know you, so is that weird? Do you prefer Taylor?

Both Tay and Taylor sounded insane and beautiful coming out of his mouth. He only had a bit of a French accent—barely noticeable. It occurred to me that I should try to say something interesting about myself.

My dentist died.

Laurent's smile faded.

Oh. I'm so sorry. That's... that sucks. That really sucks.

It's Tay. By the way. My name.

Laurent nodded with the least amount of confidence I had ever seen. He was sitting there on the gym floor just existing as a perfect specimen of mankind, while I was an alien trying to pretend that I hadn't taken over Tay's body.

I cleared my throat.

You're good. At that, I mean, the yarn? The cat thing.

He laughed.

Oh, yeah, I guess! I made them a lot in Sunday school so I figured the kids here would like them. I guess you went to a lot of Sunday school, too, yeah?

Nope. I mean yes, yeah. I did go to Sunday school. Here actually. Like, in this room. The church doesn't have a separate hall to hold this many people, so...yeah. God's cool, I guess.

He nodded again, slowly.

Yeah...yeah, God's cool.

He paused.

I'm Laurent.

I know.

Oh, you know?

No, I mean, um, I'm Tay.

I, uh...I know?

I pretended to cough but went way too far and almost threw up. Laurent covered his mouth with his hand like he was trying to be polite and not laugh. I looked around casually.

I'm gonna go. Now. Now I'm gonna go.

He asked me what my group's name was. I told him that we were the Disciples and he tried not to laugh again. He said that his group had decided on being the animals from Noah's Ark.

"Our God Is an Awesome God" ended and the preacher called out for all the kids to find their group leaders. I nodded at Laurent and turned to leave, paused, then turned back to face him again.

I, uh, I like your name! It's a nice name!

Laurent smiled.

I like your name, too.

I watched the back of Laurent's head as he walked away, and I figured that our God had to be an awesome God to create something that fucking beautiful.

The next day, I let the rain wreck my hair so that Laurent would think that I was rugged and interesting.

Since we couldn't play holy soccer baseball outside, my group and Laurent's group made a fort out of blankets in the basement of the pumphouse and huddled together to play indoor games. Jay-Lynn Munch chewed on the end of her own braid while two of the boys in my group clapped in each other's faces and claimed they were killing flies. Isaiah suggested we go around the circle and each say what we pray for in Mass. I silently prayed that the day would fucking end already.

Laurent went first. He said that he prayed for his mother. He didn't elaborate. Rowan Peterson went next and said that he prayed every night for his little brother to die in a wagon accident so Rowan could finally have his Transformers. Laurent asked him if, perhaps, he could just pray for Transformers of his own, but Rowan didn't budge.

Wyatt Brown prayed for world peace, but Joseph interrupted him and told him that was a cliché and God wants people to have original thoughts. Wyatt asked Joseph why God would make everyone follow the rules of the exact same book if he wanted to promote original thoughts, and they both turned to me for my opinion on the matter. I sighed.

God, um...wants you to give everyone else a turn first.

We kept going around in agony until Jay-Lynn paused and gave a little smirk. Let's play confession, she said.

All the kids cheered. Laurent looked at me with fear, but I just shrugged like I was cool and hip and a great church camp leader who gave the people what they wanted.

Jay-Lynn confessed with pleasure that sometimes, instead of praying to God, she prayed to the Cabbage Patch Kids 'cause she trusted them more.

A kid from Laurent's group started to cry and said that he picked a nickel up off the ground and never tried to find its owner. Lucas patted him on the back and whispered, You're forgiven, my man.

Then it was my turn. I looked at Laurent like I wanted to confess something only to him. After an awkward silence, his smile faded as if he understood. I cleared my throat.

I, uh, my mom is French...?

Isaiah shouted at me that that wasn't a real confession, and I snapped at him that my confession could be whatever I wanted it to be. I felt boring and stupid compared to the interesting kids half my age. I thought that maybe Laurent would realize how childish I was and just walk out then and there and I would never get to see his perfect cuticles up close.

Laurent hushed the kids.

My confession is that I really like Tay's confession. I think it was very confessionary.

He smiled at me again and I literally fucking died.

Later, Joseph put sunscreen on the life-sized Styrofoam nativity figurines. During our break, Laurent and I cleaned off Mary and Wise Man Number Three with our green staff sweaters. Laurent looked up at me every so often with his eyes like a kid from a Levi's commercial, and again I was struck with the urge to make myself as interesting as possible.

I took my tooth out of my pocket and held it up. This is my tooth, I said. My back molar.

Laurent looked at it curiously. He asked if I always carried a tooth in my pocket.

Not always, I said. Just this one. It's already got a hole through it so it would be cool as, like, a necklace or something. I'm acknowledging how hard teeth work and I'm carrying it like a trophy. Like, the cavity won, but my tooth still deserves to be recognized for its fight, you know?

It was the stupidest thing that I'd ever said. Laurent looked fascinated. He shuffled closer to me.

I've never gotten a cavity, he said. But I have a gap where my mom yanked out one of my baby teeth with pliers.

He smiled wide and pointed to a space between two of his teeth.

Your mom took out your tooth with pliers?

Yeah, he said matter-of-factly. What else would she have used?

I nodded even though I was confused.

Laurent moved even closer.

What if dentists have been lying to us this whole time, and fake teeth are just other people's teeth prettied up all nice?

I only half-heard him 'cause I was staring at the corners of his mouth and the little dimples just above them.

Are all teeth the same size? he asked. All grown-up teeth, I mean. Does everybody have the same sized teeth?

Open your mouth again, I said. Wait, I mean—smile. Smile is what I mean.

Laurent laughed and his laugh made me laugh. He opened his mouth.

I leaned forward so that our knees were touching. I held my molar up beside his face.

I can't tell if our teeth are the same, I said.

Laurent gently took my wrist and moved my hand closer. His fingers were warm.

Can you tell now? he asked.

I shook my head. I felt flushed, like someone had turned up the thermostat.

Laurent looked at the molar, then back at me. I hadn't noticed the freckles across his nose before. I felt sick in a good way.

Closer? he asked.

I nodded.

He covered my hand with his own and pressed them up against his cheek. His skin was burning hot. I wondered if he had a fever.

We sat like that for a full minute, just breathing and looking at each other. I couldn't remember what we had been talking about before. I couldn't even remember my name.

You smell good, I said quietly. I whispered so God wouldn't hear me.

Thanks, he said.

You're welcome, I said.

I suddenly felt embarrassed that I couldn't remember what *you're welcome* was in French. I felt embarrassed about my whole existence. He was so smart and thoughtful and I was just me and everything I'd said was garbage and he probably hated my guts.

Sorry, I said. I'm sorry. I'm sorry I showed you my tooth. I make every situation I've ever been in awkward—like this time I was out walking around at night and I walked too far and I called a cab and my driver was this guy who said that he used to be in a travelling circus with his brother and they would make this special grilled cheese with relish for good luck and I think he was joking but I believed him and I asked if he had the recipe and he didn't say anything and neither of us talked for the rest of the ride back to my house and I felt like an idiot then and I feel like an idiot now and I don't know any French and—

Can I kiss you? Laurent asked. On your forehead?

I made a face. For a second Laurent looked like he regretted opening his mouth at all.

I paused, then gave him a slow nod. He ran a hand through his hair.

Is that...yes? I just want to make sure that you want me to. On your forehead.

Uh, yeah. Yes. I'm saying yes. To the kiss.

I tried to casually lean my neck to my shoulder to smell my jacket. I wiped the sunscreen off my hands onto my pants as best I could, then shuffled onto my knees so I was sitting up straight.

Laurent looked at me like he was about to start an exam he hadn't studied for—then quickly landed a peck between my eyebrows.

He paused—looked at me for affirmation. I felt like I'd just been blessed by the fucking pope. I nodded again.

He smiled.

Maybe we could hang out, he said. Somewhere that isn't work. After work. When we aren't working.

Maybe we could, I said. Yes, I mean. Not maybe.

Not maybe, he repeated.

I thought about leaning in to kiss him properly, but he stood up and brushed himself off.

Do you want to go for a hike? he asked. This weekend?

I wanted to see him but I absolutely fucking did not want to go on a hike.

Sure! I said.

Cool. Are there any good trails around here?

Yeah, I said. For sure. For sure, yes.

I didn't really hear his question. I was too busy thinking about kissing.

He put his hand on top of mine again, but then he realized he was still covered in sunscreen and pulled away. I wasn't one of those people who didn't wash the spot where someone touched them for six months, but from that point on, I definitely started liking the smell of sunscreen.

On Saturday morning, I walked to Laurent's duplex on Lawson Road near the cove. His mother answered the door. She looked so much like Laurent that it scared me. Dark curls framed her round blue eyes.

Hi, I said. I'm here for Laurent. I work with him. With Laurent. And I'm here. For him.

She smiled that type of smile that every mom learns when they become a mom. She opened her mouth to say something, but a sharp crash interrupted her. We both turned to look through the door.

Laurent was on his knees in the foyer, sweeping shards of broken glass into his palms. I couldn't tell what he'd broken, but he was running his hands along the hardwood so fast that droplets of blood speckled the pieces of ceramic. His mother asked him something in French, too fast for me to understand. Her voice was quick and sharp.

Laurent's head snapped up. He stammered a response I couldn't quite hear. His mother turned back to face him.

I stood on the porch with my mouth shut while she got all up in his face. She talked with her whole body. Laurent didn't interrupt. His eyes tracked her hands.

The whole thing made me feel uncomfortable. My mom was annoying, but you'd never catch a tabarnak leaving her mouth unless she was on the phone with the lawyer about my lousy father's will.

Laurent's mom threw his jacket onto the ground in front of him. He flinched.

Laurent, she said, tu vas prendre la pire raclée de ta vie.

There was a pause.

D'accord, he said finally.

Laurent was silent our entire walk to the Bruce Trail. Massive squirrels picked at the Timmie's cups scattered around the overflowing garbage can at the entrance. Twisty roots jutted out of the damp dirt ground. We walked through shade so dark it seemed like night, following the trees marked with white lines along the escarpment until we reached the large flat rock that marked the halfway point. I put on Laurent's sweater and the two of us lay out on the cold stone like we were looking up at the stars.

Was your mom worried we'd get caught in the rain? I asked.

What?

Raclée means luck, right? Like, you're gonna get the worst luck?

No, he said. It doesn't.

Am I close?

Don't worry about it.

I felt like I was asking too many questions.

She's not a fan, Laurent said.

Of what?

Of me.

I wondered if it was 'cause of—you know. I didn't say anything.

She's always kind of been like that, he continued. She cares a lot about stuff, you know? And I'm not stuff anymore. I walk around and have opinions about things.

I nodded.

We walked through dense trees until forest turned to marsh. Laurent took pictures of bugs on his phone while I smiled and tried not to think about his mother. The dam in the centre of the water was covered in wet leaves. I swatted at the gnats and blackflies.

Suddenly, Laurent yanked my sleeve.

Oh my God, he said. Oh my God, I *see one*.

He pointed at the little mound of fur poking up out of the marsh water. His face was full of amazement, as if he'd never seen a fucking beaver.

I felt dizzy and confused. Every time I blinked, Maxi Miller from Boy Scouts was there instead of Laurent, but when I tried to focus my eyes on him, he was gone.

It was like my brain was a cassette tape that played everything happening in the present but sometimes memories of Maxi or my dad were recorded over the best bits of the songs—they interrupted. It was loud and disorienting and painful but it was usually manageable.

The beaver dove, slapping its tail on the water's surface. Laurent looked like he might clap.

We walked until the trees cleared. Laurent collected the stems of dandelions and tied them together into one long-ass dandelion.

Hey, I said. Does anyone ever call you Rent? You know, 'cause Lau*rent*?

I was really good at saying stupid shit.

Instead of answering, Laurent backed me up against a maple tree and took my face in his hands and kissed me right on the lips.

That first kiss was soft and slow. Then he kissed me again—a little harder, for a little longer. I felt warm and alive and terrified. I wanted to look around to make sure no one was watching us, but I didn't want to stop looking at him.

I leaned forward and kissed him back. Then I did it again. And again.

Eventually, we took a breather. He smiled and I smiled back. My hair was sticky with tree sap.

T'es beau comme un p'tit cœur.

You're calling me little?

Laurent laughed. No, no, a little *heart*. It's just an expression.

Meaning my heart is little? I asked. Like the Grinch? Should I get that checked out?

You're ridiculous, Laurent said.

I rolled my eyes.

Fine, I said. You're my little heart, too. We're both little hearts.

He balled his hand into a fist. I put both my hands overtop. I imagined we were keeping a little heart, beating beneath our palms, warm.

We started meeting up before work every morning to get bad coffee at Eggs & Things together. Laurent always bought both coffees 'cause he would get to the store before I did. He liked to be early for everything.

One morning, I got there first. The store owner, Mr. Arbour, let me sit on top of an empty blue freezer while I drank my coffee. I watched Milo Riccio buy two blue popsicles and eat them both before he got outside.

I finished my coffee, then I dumped Laurent's. It had gone cold, so I bought us two more. I sat there waiting and started picturing the two of us imaginary shopping at

Target for stuff for our imaginary apartment we would have in imaginary Washington State once we both graduated high school. Laurent would be like, *We should get an industrial shelf for the drawing room so we have somewhere to put the spider plants*, and I would be like, *Only if we also adopt an elderly hairless cat and name him Eggnog*, and we would hold hands in public 'cause everyone's accepting in Washington State and Target would have so many things that Canadian Tire doesn't have and I'd kiss him on the cheek and he'd smile and everything in our lives would be okay.

I was finishing my second coffee when the bell rang and Laurent came through the door. He walked up the aisle slowly, like he was balancing books on his head.

I hopped down off the freezer and waved at him, but he didn't wave back. He took slow, deliberate steps until he reached me.

Hi, he said quietly. His voice cracked.

Your coffee's cold, I said. You're late.

Beads of sweat trickled down his temples.

I know, he stammered. I'm sorry.

No, no, I said. I just meant—I was worried, is all.

I reached out to touch him but remembered where we were. I pulled my arm back.

I lowered my voice.

Are you okay?

Laurent shook his head. His eyes watered.

I grabbed his hand. He pulled it away.

Not here, he whispered.

I wanted to scream.

Okay, I said.

He didn't say anything. He just looked at me. His lips trembled.

On our lunch break, Laurent sat on the ground of the handi-cap stall while I cracked first-aid-kit ice packs and held them up against his back. Thick welts bloomed purple and blue and red up his spine and over both shoulders like peonies.

Your mom's a fucking witch, I said.

He said nothing.

After camp, we lay on our stomachs on the grass out front. Laurent picked two dandelions and slowly tied them together.

Do you ever think about killing yourself? he asked.

No, I lied.

Me neither, he lied.

I asked if he wanted to go back to Montreal.

No, he said.

Do you want to stay here?

No.

Do you want to go somewhere else?

His voice cracked.

I don't know.

I felt like I didn't know anything either.

We lay there until the sun set and the air chilled and the mosquitoes bit us through our clothes. Laurent rested his head in his arms.

After a while, I got an idea.

Let's pray, I said.

Laurent gave me a look. You want to…pray?

Yeah, I said, let's pray it up.

I got up onto my knees, 'cause Jesus died for me to get grass stains on my jeans. Laurent looked at me curiously, then slowly got up onto his own knees beside me.

Which prayer should we say? Laurent asked.

We're just gonna freestyle it, I said.

I clasped my hands in front of me and closed my eyes.

Hi, Father God, I started. Just you though. Like, say hi to Jesus and the Holy Ghost for me, but take me off speakerphone, if you get my drift. Anyway, hi. How are you? How was your day? Probably great. Good job with...Abel. Abel's the one who killed his brother, right?

I think so, Laurent whispered.

I nodded. Cool, yeah. Good job with Abel. That guy was a dick mouth. Also, thanks for...canned ravioli. I'm sure you made that happen. It's working out great. Anyway. This is a prayer, so like, get out a notepad. I've got a few things. One: our school only has one smartboard and we all gotta take turns with it. So a second one would be cool. Two: please make Laurent Bordeaux— Do you have a middle name?

Sebastian, Laurent said.

I nodded again. Awesome. Please make Laurent Sebastian Bordeaux—like, this one, not a different one—no, please give him Superman's skin. You know how Superman's got this super-skin so cars can hit him and shit and nothing happens, not even a scratch? Make Laurent like that. Also, like, forgive us our trespasses. I trespass a lot, especially through Centennial Park at night, 'cause it's faster even though there's a sign that says do not enter.

I turned to Laurent. Do you wanna add anything?

Laurent paused. Ask him to tell my dad that I'm doing great and I'm very happy and everyone is happy and fine. Please and thank you.

You want me to ask God to lie to your dad? I asked.

Yes, Laurent said.

I felt weird 'cause my dad was dead, too, but I didn't have any messages I wanted to pass on.

Fine, I said. Please, Father God, please flat-out lie to Laurent's dad's face. Please don't mention anything about his mom beating the shit out of him. Or about this piece-of-shit town draining the life out of his beautiful, beautiful body. Also, don't mention that time we stayed late after camp and drank a whole box of communion wine and messed around on the chancel.

Taylor.

What? It's not like he doesn't know. He's around us literally all the time.

A pause.

Are you going to pray for anything for yourself? Laurent asked.

I already asked for the smartboards.

I mean, something just for you.

I couldn't use the thing I usually prayed for, 'cause if God decided that he finally wanted to answer me, I wouldn't feel the way I did about Laurent. Love fucking blows.

Say hi to Maxi, I said. And Dr. Dan.

I moved my tongue around the gap where my molar used to be. Laurent's eyes stayed closed; his fingers interlocked so tightly, his knuckles turned white. I watched him closely. I wondered if there was such a thing as a second-hand miracle.

Laurent and I sat in the back pew at Mass together the next Sunday. It only took until halfway through the first hymn for the metre between us to shrink to an inch.

During the passing of the peace, I slipped a plastic baggie into his hand. He opened it while the other congregation members closer to the front went up for their communion.

My tooth sat in his palm. I'd threaded a piece of pink yarn through the hole the cavity had made.

Laurent put the necklace on and laid his head on my shoulder.

Would you leave with me, he asked, if you could?

I held my breath and scanned the pews around us. People were staring. I let them.

Yeah, I said.

Laurent looked at me like he understood. We both knew this was a place that didn't let people leave. We weren't going to be the exception to that rule.

We closed our eyes.

And we tried and failed to pray ourselves out of The Pump.

HOME

We were in the cramped-ass Mercury Villager going eighty an hour on Highway 10 from the Falls back to The Pump, and my mother was trying to convince me to go to conversion therapy.

She said she knew a guy—not like a robed-up, pew-obsessed raisin of a dude who shoves Jesus crackers into the mouths of little boys—but, like, a *normal guy*, like he even grew up in Orangeville and our old neighbour knew him and she only knows legit guys, so, like, he must be legit. He just talks to people, not like a freaking shrink or anything like that. You just talk and you can, like, tell him all the shit you're afraid to tell me—like if Mr. Wallace from the Y put his hand in your panties or something when you were, like, five—and you can talk about it so you can get better. You can even wear a beanie until your hair grows back. Your hair was so pretty when it was long, Joanne.

It didn't feel shitty or anything, not even a little bit, not even, like, at all. I was fine. I let her do her spiel while Kim Mitchell played on the radio and I nodded and agreed to grow out my hair. I told her it was because I liked it long, too, but really I just thought it would be hot if I had a long-ass ponytail my girlfriend Marty could pull on while we were in bed.

We drove for thirty minutes and out of the Greenbelt until, surprise: the hunk of metal on wheels broke the fuck down. Mom kept the radio volume all the way up while she called CAA. I doubted they could hear her even a little bit. Kim Mitchell was really killing it, like, really working magic with his fucked-up rockin' vocal cords. I imagined a massive-ass jumbo jet falling from the sky and destroying our car like in the movie *Knowing* with Nic Cage.

I slammed open the sliding door and went to sit on the gravel shoulder. Mom yelled at me to get back in the car before I got hit by a transport truck and died. I yelled back that if I got hit by a transport truck, maybe only the dyke part of me would die.

Marty talked about death a lot. She said the more you talked shit about something the less it mattered. When we first started dating, we left her little brother's funeral early to sit in the parking lot of Mr. Desperate's and wrote each other's obituaries.

We read them out loud for the other to hear. I went first.

> *Marty Miller was always...unsure...but... she's really dead now, folks, she's gone. She's, like, really certainly dead, dead dead dead and honestly, God bless her. She's not having an open casket because she—she wanted to be ashes? So you can, like, go see them...the ashes...in the lake or whatever. That's what she would want. Which is depressing as fuck, but she was just a person. She wasn't, like, a poet or artist or anything so that's what she gets. So yeah, um, thank you for coming.*

I thought it sucked, but Marty cried and said it was the best thing she'd ever heard about herself.

Marty wrote my obituary on a napkin and told me to read it when I was alone later that night:

> *In loving memory of an old self. They told everyone they were allergic to pond water. They ate playdough because of that one Robert Munsch book. They refused to go into the Bay because of the butterfly-shaped spotlights covering the tile floor. They swallowed the first baby tooth they lost—they got the quarter anyway. They were often photographed wearing checkered yellow overalls. They leave behind the following: a collection of broken rubber bands; the notion that mismatched socks are good luck; a time capsule, opened the day after it was buried; an unwavering trust in adults; female pronouns.*
>
> *Their presence will sit on playground slides; initials in sidewalks; the old rainbow streamer Skip-It in their mother's garage.*

Mom sat in the passenger seat and said that CAA would come in an hour. I ate the warm Joe Louis from my pocket. She shouted over the radio and all I heard was something about rot. She turned the radio off.

Have you given it any thought?

What?

The therapy.

Mm-hmm.

Well, have you?

WELL, not really.

She said I should take my time to decide, since it was private and wasn't covered by insurance. It would probably cost her, like, a ton. She took out her phone and said she'd made a list in her notes app of things she thought might be making me think I was gay and that I wasn't a girl—they do this kind of thing in therapy. I read that on Yahoo! It's like Freud's repression, that kind of stuff.

In order, they were:

> 1. Your elementary school friend's babysitter who had kind of big breasts, and sometimes wore low-cut clothes and ripped jeans.

> 2. The time when I didn't know what to get you for Christmas so I went to Sunrise and they recommended *So Jealous* by those girls Tiki and Sara and for a while it was the only CD you put in that damned player.

> 3. The thing with your dad. You know.

> 4. I let you watch a lot of *Sailor Moon*.

It was fine because I didn't even laugh or, like, anything. I just told her she was probably right and that Freud was right and that I really wish I wasn't so tempted by the Sailor Scouts.

An hour passed. Mom said that I was gonna get dirty if I kept sitting in the gravel. I pretended I couldn't hear her.

After another half-hour, I said I could call Marty to come pick us up.

Who?

Marty.

Marta?

MARTY.

Your friend Marty?

My friend Marty.

And what do Marty's parents do?

I sighed and called her anyway.

Marty parked her stepdad's mint-green truck behind us on the shoulder. She was wearing black leggings and my jean jacket with the patch I'd sewn on the sleeve that read *Death to gender*. She introduced herself to my mom and shook her hand all official-like, as if my mom totally didn't want us to burn in hell. We all shoved into the truck. I tried to Google Map the closest chop shop while Marty answered my mom's fucked-up questions.

Is Marty short for Martha?

Uh, no. It's actually just Marty.

That's a boy's name, you know. Do your parents know that Marty is a boy's name?

They like Michael J. Fox a lot. It's Marty like Marty McFly, like from *Back to the Future*?

Oh—well, I've never seen that. It's still a boy's name, you know.

We drove to a truck-stop diner called the Sixth Wheel and sipped on burnt coffee while a tow truck finally recovered the Villager. Marty and I sat opposite my mother like we were at an interview or some shit. Mom asked Marty about the upcoming municipal elections. Jacob Jameson's been around for a couple cycles now and he's just been doing just fine, she said. Why change what's been doing fine?

He raised our water bills, Marty said, and none of us can even take a shower.

My mother scoffed. What do the *millennials* expect him to do—give everything out for free?

It's *water*.

Money doesn't fall from the sky, honey.

Water *literally* falls from the sky.

Let's talk about something else, I interrupted.

Okay, Marty said, turning toward my mother. Jo tells me that you hate gay people?

My mother made a face.

I don't ha— that's such a— I don't hate anybody. I'm not homophobic.

So you're fine with the fact that I'm a raging homosexual.

Dear, you can do whatever you want with your life.

Because I'm not your kid.

I'm sorry, sweetie, do *you* have kids? Are you a *mother*? Have you carried the seed of life within your heart and then nursed it at your *bosom*?

I literally could not think of something more nauseating.

Marty got up and excused herself to the washroom. She took one look at the line in front of the women's stalls and walked right into the men's. Mom looked sick.

Did she just—did she—

Please just chill out, Mom.

I swished the coffee around my gums like mouthwash. My mother cleared her throat.

So.

So...

What are you thinking? About the therapy?

Nothing really.

That's all you have to say about it? Nothing really?

I guess so.

You guess so.

Can this wait until we're home?

You're overthinking it. You overthink everything—that's why you're so confused all the time. It would be nice for you to get out of town for a bit.

Marty and I had been talking a few days before about leaving on our own trip, but, like, the kind of trip where you get the fuck out and never ever come back. Marty had suggested we go to Toronto because of how cultured it was. They even have a gay village and everything, she'd said.

I asked her why all the gay people only stayed in one part of the city and she assured me that it wasn't, like, by law or anything. It was cool and hip like San Francisco. She said that she already had money from her pioneer village gig to put a deposit on a basement apartment. I'd never really left The Pump except to go to Beaverton to visit Grandad and his wife, who Mom said I wasn't allowed to call Grandma under any circumstances or so help her God she'd send me to live with Uncle Rick downtown. Uncle Rick could've helped us find a place, no doubt, because he knew the city like he drew it up himself, but he also asked *Where's my hug?* a little too often, and then there was that thing with him playing doctor. Not that I remembered anyway. Not like it mattered.

When Marty had asked about leaving, I hadn't really known whether to say yes or no or that I wasn't sure. I felt like I was attached to The Pump by a shitty extension cord, and if I tried to drift too far away, the universe would set me the fuck straight and zap the life out of me.

Marty came back and insisted she pay for the coffee . My mother pulled money out of her purse so fast that the bills almost ripped. We all went out into the parking, where the mechanics had left the Villager.

Before Marty left to get into her truck, she grabbed the back of my head and kissed me like I was fresh fruit. Like, she really went for it, she really took a full bite out of me. She drove off without a word.

My mother didn't talk the whole ride back to The Pump. She gripped the steering wheel like we were dangling off a cliff and if she loosened her grip we'd be insta-corpses, which honestly wouldn't have been a bad way to bookend our shitshow of a day.

Marty and I met up at the salt dome beside the cop shop later that night. I brought extra socks, because last time we made the trek, half the forest trail off Maple Street flooded and green water soaked through my Giant Tiger knock-off Uggs and Marty's Docs. We scrubbed our feet raw with Magic Erasers that night. We didn't want any extra toes or other shit.

People stopped using The Pump's two salt domes before Marty and I were born. The Mayor left all the barbed wire fences and shit up, but we could sneak onto the property if we curled up the bottom of the fence and got flat on our stomachs and army-crawled under. The trees stopped after the fence, and we frolicked through a soccer field's worth of wood chips till we got to the dome itself.

Inside, wet rafters rotted against the curved wooden walls. When the dome was operational, there would've been a big-ass pile of salt in the centre for us to climb and then toboggan down on garbage-can lids and shit, but now the remaining salt just covered the floor in a thin layer. One time, Marty went home without rinsing her boots off in the lake first and her family's cocker spaniel licked them non-stop.

She'd learned from that night though. Now she left her Docs in the wood chips and walked through the dome in the striped green *Cops are pigs* socks she bought online. I left my sneakers on. Marty yelled *Suck my pussy* as loud as she could. The dome answered back in a fading echo. *Pussy. Pussy. Pussy.*

We filled a dental dam with salt and tied it at the top with a hair elastic and used it as a hacky sack. Then we lay on the ground and made salt angels. Marty added a backpack to her angel with her finger and poked little holes where her Green Party pins would be. I gave my angel eyes, but then thought that was stupid and wiped them away. I'd already seen enough for both the angel and me.

I'm a witch, Marty said.

She sat up and did criss-cross apple sauce like you do in kindergarten.

Oh, I said. How did you find out? You didn't pay for Ancestery.com right? That shit's a rip-off.

No, Marty said. I didn't have to find out. I just decided I am one. Just now.

Oh, I said again. That's kind of hot.

We should do a hex tonight, she said. On Jacob Jameson.

Sure, I said. I don't have any data left on my phone though. You'll have to google it on yours.

No, Marty said. No googling. We can make our own. First we'll draw a circle in the salt—

Don't you need a circle *of* salt though?

And then we'll sing our ABCs backwards, in unison, then we'll make love in the circle, then we'll only drink Coke Zero for a whole month.

That sounds complicated.

Justice is complicated, Jo.

I shrugged. I didn't know anything about magic anyway.

We only got as far as drawing the circle, because Marty brought out the two-litre bottle of Coke Zero and vodka she'd brought in her backpack and we got too sloshed to do the ABCs. Marty's laugh rose three hundred octaves when she drank vodka, which always made me laugh and her laugh and me laugh and her laugh until we couldn't breathe.

We were laughing like that, all loud and contagious, until Marty took a swig, sighed, and said that I should call Child Protective Services on my mother.

What? I asked. Why? She just runs her mouth.

She wants you to pray the gay away, Marty said. And she won't use your pronouns. That's literally abuse.

Bullshit, I said. She doesn't smack me around.

I'm not saying that, she said. But it's still fucked-up, Jo.

I didn't understand where Marty was coming from. Even though my mother was queen of all the fucked-up loud-mouth-fake-ass Southern Ontario Belle Bitches, it was obvious she wasn't trash. You had to be food-stamp poor *and* beat the living shit out of your kids to be considered trash in The Pump. Like Ed Sampson, who painted his kids purple and blue right up until the Rash got one and the beavers got the other. Ed Sampson was trash. Or Taylor Levesque, whose mom always sat beside my mom at Sunday service. Taylor's pretty boyfriend got the shit kicked out of him every other day, it looked like, but Mrs. Levesque said that Linda Miller said that Eliza Kilber said that Winifred Michaels said that Marie Bordeaux paid her duplex deposit in cash, one of those places in the new subdivision on Lawson where the sidewalks are chalk white, so they don't qualify as trash.

She's not a bad mom, I said. She—she doesn't understand, like...she's, um—she's not bad. She's not.

You probably only think that because you have Stockholm Syndrome.

You're being a bitch.

Marty threw her hands up.

Fucking fine then, she said. I'm sorry. I'm sorry as fuck that I love you and that loving you makes me a fucking piece of shit and that your ass-lips, Republican, granny-pussy mom is *dousing your queer fire* and you *like it* and that she voted for a lying piece of shit-corn who'd rather jail his own kid than clean our fucking water. I'm sorry you'd rather drop out and get a job at Eggs & Things part-time and let your second cousin knock you up and raise your fucked-up cousin-babies and throw *them* into conversion therapy and never fucking leave this shithole of a town.

I said nothing.

Fuck, Jo, I'm sorry, she said. I'm as bad as your mom now. Worse. You can break up with me if you want. I'll understand. I will.

I wanted to ask Marty what the fuck the problem was with wanting to live in the town you were born in. I wanted to ask her why working at Eggs & Things and having babies made you a shitty person. Normal was talking gossip about your neighbours at the cash while you bought microwave dinners, letting your Tory mother tell you to grow your hair out, pretending to pray when you were really just resting your eyes, and losing your mind when the township finally put a Timmies on Main and it was predictable and it was safe and it was fine. Maybe I wasn't supposed to do better than fine. Maybe that was okay.

It's alright, I said. I forgive you.

I grabbed the Orange Crush bottle and took a swig. I wondered if my mother's God knew how much of a liar I was.

Marty found an attic apartment in a duplex in the Annex a month later. I helped her pack her favourite shirts and pins and her great-grandfather's penny collection in a green canvas army bag that was taller than she was. We took the tacks out of the old movie tickets on her bulletin board and packed them in cardboard boxes with her school pictures and Polly Pockets and every piece of beach glass she had ever found. We piled everything in her entryway, then sat on her kitchen floor and ate icing from the container with spoons.

Mrs. Miller sat in a forest-green La-Z-Boy in the living room and nursed a glass of warm orange juice with pulp. She stared at the wallpaper.

I'm taking Maxi's Scout sash, Marty said loud enough for her mother to hear.

She got no reply.

Mom, I'm taking the sash with me, Marty repeated. Maxi's. I'm taking it. To Toronto.

Mrs. Miller sipped her juice.

Marty snorted. Whatever—fuck talking, I guess.

Marty walked into her mother's bedroom and emerged with a folded green sash.

I went home for dinner so Marty could spend her final moments in her childhood bedroom alone to think those fucked-up alone-people thoughts that everybody has but nobody talks about. I told my mother I was meeting Marty at the Greyhound stop on Main at 9:00 p.m. so I could see her off safely.

Mom was nervously chatty. She moved her scalloped potatoes around her plate but never took a bite.

Does Martha have renter's insurance yet? she asked. She'll need that, you know. Kids are always forgetting things like that.

It's *Marty*, Mom. *Mar-tee.*

How's her credit? If she doesn't have good credit she'll get kicked out and she'll have to move to one of those neighbourhoods that smells like a Goodwill store.

Mom.

Does she have a park nearby? She'll go bananas if she doesn't have a patch of green somewhere to escape to. Do you remember when we used to go on walks down by the marshes? Do you remember how you used to run around in the mud and tell me that the beavers were talking to you?

For the love of God, Mom, just shut the fuck up.

Silence. Mom's gaze went down to her lap.

Do you...do you have good memories? Mom asked. From when you were small? You do, don't you? Like our walks, right? You remember the walks?

It struck me that my mom only knew how to be the mother I needed back then and that she had literally no idea how to be the mother I needed now.

I looked at her and she looked like me.

I'm not going to the therapy, I said.

She sat still for a moment, then nodded.

We could go for a walk after dinner, she said. If you wanted to do that. Like how we used to. It's late. The beavers should be sleeping by now.

I can't, I said. I have to meet Marty. At nine, remember?

She looked at me a little too long. Maybe she knew that I was leaving. Maybe she didn't. I've never asked her. I doubt I ever will.

Yes, she said. Yes, I remember.
She smiled.
That was our last conversation.

Marty and I chose the back seats on the Greyhound, right above the wheels. She leaned her head against my shoulder and fell asleep before we even left the stop. She clutched her backpack like a teddy bear.

The driver shut off the aisle lights and we drove down the length of Main. I saw a black van parked with its hazards on while we were stopped at a red light on Christie Road, and I expected my mother to wave from the window as if she had followed me to say goodbye. But when I looked again, it wasn't a Mercury Villager at all.

The light turned green and we continued onto the highway on-ramp. I turned a few times in my seat to see the hazards of the almost-Villager flashing on and off at the road's edge. The farther we drove, the softer the blinking light became. Eventually, it was just an orange dot in a sea of dark, like a lighthouse beacon cutting through a storm. Like we were on a ship leaving home.

Your mother leaves The Pump. There is nothing left for her here. Not now.

She sells the redwood china cabinet and the torn leather couch and your childhood toys at a yard sale on the front lawn the Saturday before she skips town. Your blue-and-green Fisher-Price kitchen doesn't sell. She takes the toy kitchen and her mother's china and eleven garbage bags of clothes and drops them off at the Sally Ann.

She packs whatever is left into her brother's Villager: yellow disposable cameras filled with undeveloped film, your kindergarten artwork, boxes of old TV remotes and broken sculptures and VHS tapes and unopened Bibles and canned food for your lost cat.

On her way out of The Pump, your mother pulls off the service road and parks the van at the entrance to the marshes. The sky is black—no stars. She rolls down the windows, and the frogs and crickets scream a symphony. She cranes her neck, looking out into the tall pines and muddy water. She looks for the beavers.

They were here first, but The Pump does not belong to them. The Pump belongs to people. Dead trees sit stacked in unfinished construction sites, bound together by metal wire. Mud hardens at the base of the riverbed behind the Jameson Inc. industrial buildings. They pump chemicals into the water, day and night. Tar and concrete flatten the places the dams should be. Everything is touched by humans—fleshy and fragile, boisterous and greedy.

Only the marshes are left. Water striders sink into thick sludge. The air hums like a television set. All things stick to one another.

Your mother sees puffs of breath escape out the top of the massive lodge, built not with sticks but human bones. She almost hears the family inside. She almost hears their conversation. Layers of mud. Slick fur swimming through reeds from the chamber to the pond. Tails smack the water top. A splash.

There's one first. Then many. Green ripples hit the mossy rocks. Shadows stitch the dark water. Your mother sits still while the water sways.

They have known nothing other than The Pump, but it is time for them to leave. One has this idea first. It tells the others.

Your mother sits in the van and watches the beavers for hours. Day breaks and the grey clouds begin to clear. She sits and watches as all of them leave the water.

They run through dense trees and across the soft ground. Acorn bits wedge between their toes. They do not look back as they run. They are not afraid of losing one another. They know where to go. They cannot stay in The Pump any longer.

When the last of the beavers is gone, your mother steps out of the van and walks to the edge of the road's shoulder. She stops a foot before the water.

She kneels in the gravel and sinks her hands into the marshy mud. Her skin stings. The water turns her palms bright red but she does not mind. She wants to remember later. The smell. The pain.

She drives away. I do not know where she goes. Not to her father in the States. Not to her brother in the city. It is somewhere she has never been before now. Somewhere else.

ACKNOWLEDGEMENTS

The Pump would not exist without the eyes, guidance, patience, and support of many people in my life. I owe the most thanks to my professor, undergraduate thesis supervisor, mentor, and dear friend Tom Cull, who has fought for this collection since its inception in 2017. Thank you to Michael Fox, who served as my second reader while the collection was still a thesis project. Thank you to Jonathan Hermina, Brianne Henderson, Kassidy Gallina, and Laura Brooks, who let me read them terrible first drafts of these stories while we all should have been studying for our exams.

I am so grateful and so lucky that Andy Verboom and Kailee Wakeman originally took a chance on my weird little book, and that Invisible Publishing took that same chance when I needed it most. To *The Pump*'s first editor, Annick MacAskill: this collection is what it is because of you. Thank you.

Thank you to the *Gateway Review*, which published an earlier version of "Pelargonia"; *Coffin Bell*, which published an earlier version of "Vellum"; *Thorn Literary Magazine*, which published an earlier version of "Life Giver"; and *American Chordata*, which published an earlier version of "Mal aux Dents." Thank you to Francesca Ekwuyasi and the *Malahat Review* for selecting an earlier draft of "The Bottom" for the 2020 Open Season Awards shortlist.

Thank you to the brilliant Camille Intson, who is my biggest cheerleader.

Thank you to my love Christian Hegele, who is my partner in all things. He is the Laurent to my Tay.

Most of all, thank you to my mother Martina, my father David, and my brother Jakob. We do our best with what we have, and we have each other, so we'll do our best.

Sydney Hegele (formerly Sydney Warner Brooman) is the winner of the 2022 ReLit Literary Award for Short Fiction and a finalist for the 2022 Trillium Book Award. Their poetry chapbook *The Last Thing I Will See Before I Die* is forthcoming from 845 Press in 2022. They live with their husband and French Bulldog in Toronto, Canada. *The Pump* is their first book.

INVISIBLE PUBLISHING produces fine Canadian literature for those who enjoy such things. As an independent, not-for-profit publisher, our work includes building communities that sustain and encourage engaging, literary, and current writing.

Invisible Publishing has been in operation for over a decade. We released our first fiction titles in the spring of 2007, and our catalogue has come to include works of graphic fiction and nonfiction, pop culture biographies, experimental poetry, and prose.

We are committed to publishing diverse voices and experiences. In acknowledging historical and systemic barriers, and the limits of our existing catalogue, we strongly encourage writers from LGBTQ2SIA+ communities, Indigenous writers, and writers of colour to submit their work.

Invisible Publishing is also home to the Bibliophonic series of music books and the Throwback series of CanLit reissues.

If you'd like to know more, please get in touch: info@invisiblepublishing.com